I0670903

Mirach Speaks
To His
Grammatical Transparents

Will Alexander

MIRACH SPEAKS
TO HIS
GRAMMATICAL TRANSPARENTS

by Will Alexander

OYSTER
MOON
PRESS
BERKELEY, CALIFORNIA

Mirach Speaks To His Grammatical Transparents
by Will Alexander

Front cover illustration: *Inside the Methane Monsoon*, by the author.
Back cover illustration: *Listening at Higher Scale*, by the author.

The author wishes to thank Tetra Balestri for transcribing the manuscript.

ISBN: 978-0-578-08445-9

Additional copies of this book can be ordered from LuLu:
http://www.lulu.com

Oyster Moon Press is a non-profit, surrealist publishing co-op located in
Berkeley, California.

http://www.oystermoonpress.com

"...Islamic astronomers went far beyond Greek mathematical methods and provided essential tools for the creation of Western Renaissance astronomy."

-Oxford Astronomy Encyclopedia

"...in each and every one of the infinite number of universes, there are an infinite number of variegated planets."

Bhaktivedanta Swami
-Easy Journey to Other Planets

CONTENTS

Introduction: On Intuitive Primevals................9

Mirach Speaks To His Grammatical Transparents................11

Mirach: Inaugural Electrification Part I................15

Mirach: Inaugural Electrification Part II................19

Mirach: Strategic Electrifications Parts I-VII................21

El Nath: On Huertas................63

El Nath: The Immeasurable Number As Wave................65

El Nath: On Inaugural Formality................69

Aludra: On Anonymous Energy................73

Bellatrix: On Auras, Hydroxyl and Saturn................129

Altair: On Sculpting Hydroxyl................137

Alnitak: On Susurrant Conveyance and Yield................139

The Sun 141

Glossary................143

On Intuitive Primevals

These lectures are texts, are stars, are energies, uttering intuitive primevals. They translate from a scale which hails from in-human fervour, bringing to a pitch the dialectical context of the Sun and the Earth, the latter persisting under the pressure of European mechanization, and the psycho-physical ailments which befall the aforesaid mechanization active as post-industrial effects.

Because such misalignment presently occurs, it infects the Sun. And because of this infection the Sun has become de-centred and aimless. Illness exists in its rays. A Federation of suns led by the star Mirach listens to its struggles and comes to its aid in order to restore its spiritual health, and by extension human psychosensory oscillation. Which is simultaneous with the Earth's motility, its unprecedented balance evinced through the electrifying range of its flora and fauna.

Each star retains its Arabic nomen. (All terms followed by an asterisk are described in greater detail in the glossary.) Their spirit is what we would call in present times the right brain. Which means they seep from those internalities which we know fueled the Nile Valley, and formed the universal powers which spawned the powers that formed Moorish Andalusia. They always point to the neo-alchemic of the Earthly cellular structure, always advancing from their spirit the wealth of interior ascendance.

They collectively invigorate the art of nutation so as to shift the Earth ever so slightly away from the forces of the unseen, who repetitively serve the expenditure of rays which know no other power than death. Their generosity and insistence points to the yield of a higher order.

-Will Alexander

Mirach Speaks To His Grammatical Transparents

For now I will not state any numerical design to the cosmos. I will only elicit carbon as one of its ellipses or possibilities. As you grope with your present stages of duration, with your interpersonal transparencies, I need not remind you that you ambulate by means of the power of your internal carbon. For instance, the subconscious craft of dreaming, all the while dreaming, all the while rising from its secondary depth into the world of visible events, while still excelling further above various sub-quanta into higher concealment. And I am not speaking of any Freudian mazes, or any attempt at containment in terms of a prone or dialectical reasoning. First, one must continue to feel that the void is burning, that its script remains in shadow, in order to organically inhale the documents of one's inheritance. In this regard the family tree must remain as a singular note without any zoomorphic or astrological importance. It remains a triangular in-specific. It must not hound you, or inhere in your hands' stiflings, or misgivings which deter you in margins holding the plaintiff's deck of cards. You must resist what I consider a negligible tendency which alters the inchoate, the splendiferous, always seeking the explanatory notions of why you suddenly exist. These notions are always seeking a purely conscious distance from the explosive letters kindled in your mystery.

For instance, at a certain point in circular time I never stood on carbon, or argued from its base for monological regularity inside the act which is known as breathing. Because this remains my imminence, it cannot be concluded that I speak from angelic quanta, or from descending puzzles structured on the motifs of demons. But if it is true that mental structures burn, I want to feel their osmosis, their tinctured meanderings other than monology. Within this spirit I want to explore the hidden text. The text which is rendered by means of its hiddenness. Its hiddenness which remains alive beyond a paralytic visibility.

For me, the phoneme is spore, is flotational mist from the outer lakes of space. In your writing I will ask you to inhabit the lingering inceptions as they exist in the primordia of Io or Triton. Then give me the instants induced in your minds when they explore the basic principles of Saturn, the hydroxyl, then the infinite remains of the galaxy. Do not confine yourself to wind, to oceans set ablaze by the maladjusted cinders of the Sun. Know that the phoneme is drift, that the key to one's enigma is not the poetic rivalrous stockade, nor to a storm of dulled political misnomers. No. We are looking at something beyond the black and deaf horses of Homer, beyond the trace amount of blood which both provokes and unnerves Virgil. As for Dante, we will no longer pursue the stagnant corpses of the ancients. No. No longer a parochial kind of cosmos where the letters re-circulate as iron. True, there is a source for origins in this work, but what can be gathered is a triune manipulation of war, of agony contiguous to agony. A paradigm of Sparta and Christ. The agon, the delirious elixirs of fear. Juggled depths, partial dimensions epically stated. These are not the crafts that we seek to combine. For instance, if one of you breaks through his fear and announces a new green sun 20 billion years into the future this is one recognition of the void experienced in the palpable domain. Such writing would also advance mercurial longevity, this being a writing which ignites a recognition beyond cunning disputation. One then begins to stray above the partial dialectics of the void. Let us enunciate our powers within its partial locales. This is what I'll call the conundrum of Ernst Mach,* where shadows of brilliance are pushed by the fingers. Infinite motion is transmuted, the constellations suddenly shift according to rotational nutation.

Let us go further. Picture your attempts to conjure a being from the lower inhabitants of Earth. Say, an eel with the contrasting gifts of several sovereign emotions. And I'm equating these emotions with the auspices of hunger and graft, under the compelling remonstrance which evinces itself as screaming. This is merely one example or litmus. Maybe a recipe of verbs for lianas, or cecropias, or almonds. or perhaps an aural surge of sawdust mountains scattered near the borders of Tibetan plateaus.

Let me ask this gathering collectively, how would you imply these measures, say, in psychic viharas, or access reflections from mirrors inside your scriptings? Or course I'm asking this rhetorically, yet I am serious concerning the spirit inside your written conveyance. And by conveyance I mean the implantation of letters on a page. And by letters, I mean the phonemes, the dots, the sovereign streaks inside the alphabet. This is the level of hearing one requires. The many paths to the phonemes, the many blends of the words into phrases.

Let me say that I am not seeking from you a geometric ballast, a superficial harmonization according to your grasp of Pollux,* or Deneb,* of Beta Centauri.* I am not measuring you according to trampled foliage or cinder, or by a superficial skill gained by the raptures contained in scientific foment. I cannot gauge you by the rules as captured by someone else's dishonour. None of this applies at this hour, because I am only seeding the scope which spins inside the scope of your inherent transparencies.

I do not hope to impose an amorphic interblending, or present to you a strain of immeasurable sub-surfaces to suddenly test yourselves so as to prove your worth to a moribund community. Because it must be acknowledged that what exists around us is nothing other than a psychic swamp, nothing other than a gloomy oasis. This is the hazard that we face as cosmic igniters, as transparent grammarians, as curious solstice workers. We pronounce the matter of fact as askewment, as the sum of panicked multitudes as means. These are the ramparts of soldiers and murderers, of sentiment graft exchangers, of political mobs bent on destroying the meticulous. Therefore our understanding of charisma is always living at the source which kindles our transparency.

In closing, let me speak of the elevated tree, the scope which includes as phantasmic lunation certain splinterings which are called Aldebaran,* Altair*, Antares.* I call these the stars of blue soil. Then let me speak of Procyon* as nimbus, as cataract which shifts in the storm of new thoughts, to see results in a purposeful chromium. As I once again enrapture the hail inside your nothingness, let me once again give you an ark of blue suns burning in the core of the depths, seeking out the strategies weaving themselves inside the riddles of dangerous waters.

Mirach: Inaugural Electrification Part I

We left off in the midst of the uttering of flame. Perhaps a traceable index or phantom. Perhaps a burst of lariats in the heavens. Or forces concerned with the stationary eye struggling with trans-rotation. Take the impure process of lightning on Saturn. There are sparks conceived by at least 12 of its moons; then nothing. Not even the chemicals compounded in a flameless alpine lizard which seems to monstrously function and at the same time magnetically de-comply. This is not to say that infinity carries difference, or moves in the way that various suns emit their rays scorching or imploding their peregrinations. Since infinity exists it does vary, it does complexify and rotate, and again, if I told you that the Sun drifts, that the Sun we've come to sustain suggests itself with illness, you need to infer from this that it suffers from sustained decimations incited by decimal staggerings in Greek, which points to an inferno of wizened symbols cut off from their Nilotic origins.

We've come to re-recognize the hemispheric South, to listen to its Rams, its cereals, its spirit. As suns we are non-compliant with ice and its less conclusive principles. Of course you are beginning to understand that I speak by vibrational apparition. I speak by codes in the higher sub-text of hearing so that there is both fervour and invigoration, clairaudiance and insurrection. We have come to provoke a lessened territorial ether. A less provincial substratum which re-spawns itself allowing our ailing brother to re-focus his electroluminescence, his tribophosphorescence so that the equinox en-springs a luminous field of gullies. Then birds reverse their solemn exposure to default. All previous paradoxicals are restored. Can you see that I am shifting beyond fixation and fixation, beyond fixed system and fixed system? We who have arisen from poltergeist pontoons, from ordinal systems of Earth, and Saturn, and Mars, we understand how blizzards and death exchange themselves, and supersede themselves, considered from the view of a concussive yet intangible verdigris. Because we view the oceans as a meteoritic rain a billion kilometers deep by understanding their power in being spawned in aboriginal deafness. As parallels we can think of galactic condensation on Io, or pluperfect waters lapping the shores of Olympus Mons.* These are awesome interactions between Mars and Earth, and Io, and Saturn. In your galactic transition this can only be experienced as a fraction of your hearing, as corrupted pores of local transcription. And I grant that they are magnitudes never implied by zones which exist beyond anti-conception. By being veiled you carry inside your workings the very power of the anti-conceptive. Of course you know that you hear, your audition is rife, is the one true element which over-reaches itself as waves of light which co-erupt from the human soma. In the blue soil of the cosmos there exist the coils of evolutive vibration, a magically condensed furnace, where spells proceed as if a hawk were siphoning elements from different colours on Triton. This is not to say that a specific orange will blaze, or that a tree will reconfigure as atomic confusion. Such examples are only the beginning of your settlement and leanings. I can only think of Divine castigation and magic.

If I'm seen as glass, as a window to new infernos, listen; when the moons under this ailing aegis utter, listen. It is a concerto of the insolvent, a cryptographic inflammation given over to the language of terminal incensement. Then re-receive your-selves as this blank incensement by conveying a tumultuous strength in your peripheral intuition. Understand, by your very being you have transcended the gravity of dearth by your presence. You have brought to a phenomena a grasp of stinging tools, a dissected unification feeding your verbs with open combinations of enigma. Therefore, I cannot allow you to think in terms of old Croatian voids, or in the sourceless molecules of flags. You are open to rescue and achievement by rescue, your fuels now taking on the sigils of the sealed book, the unfamiliar contemplation, you being clairaudients, kamarupas,* pretersensuals, burning by mysterious organics.

Mirach: Inaugural Electrification Part II

We exist as part of the preternatural. We are giant quanta as ghosts. So under the present anomaly we are fish who stagger over land as if we took on the trait of human perambulation. We are the dialectic named between flight and ground. We are incendiary magnets. We are exploded conceptual fields, carrying a maniacal fecundity which influences all natural law as it currently exists in a free-standing ledger. Since we know that the bulk of instants burns, we absorb and re-emit all the histories according to verbal relay as schism. So, for instance, if I leave a mark within a dazzling trail of misnomer, if I linger around the form of a pre-existent speech, it is only to derive skills which both summon and vanish, allowing conveyance beyond a geriatric ringing prone to drift inside a feckless conservation. Maybe a tumbling through Iberian soils, or a dislocated gulf transmixed with the Aegean. There is never a thirst for common admixture, or for transcriptions fused with the scripture of mundane recording. Only the fantastic lingers, only biological metamorphism which creates in its depths a trigonometric key which fuels vertiginous alchemic reversal. Thus, you must resist these fuels and inhabit them until your essence takes flight through dis-inhabited transcendence. As these new occulted solar masses, we possess savagery through skill by osmosis. We are vehicular cinders, not light implied by didactic mirage. We do not take up integers in towers, simply to announce ourselves as a repeatable roundelay or collective. When your light flashes forth, consider bursts in the atmosphere, consider signs, consider the core of your insurrectional strengths. These are turnings, these are structures which descend half, by insurrectional half. First of all you cannot see yourselves, and at the same time adjust your self-acuities to self-perceiving events. Not spell by technocracy, not by a culminate or extrinsic distance which disembodies soil. This is not a strict or inconceivable achievement, but an adroitness, a verbal sorcery of expression. With the present plutocracy slowly cooking in its prism, we mesh with the force of explosive seething, which in turn cedes its remnants to weightless myrioramas. Which become in themselves thermal momentums, rays, power at the source of its brightness. Because light is conveyed through blindness, through sudden thought transmission, which repeats inside the soul at all angles.

Mirach: Strategic Electrifications Part I

What I say is certainly not approached by storms attached to the millenarian, or thought enhanced as if I stood amongst you as an unnamed Pantocrater.* Not engendering a fast, or igniting solar executions, I remain outside of any religious or equational grasp. True, I understand that arks burn, that citizens fray and settle in on themselves as anarchic implosives. I don't debate this. But what I do in my mind is always an attempt to cast the illimitable, seeing in each circle of scorpions, pion after pion of scorching visual dice. By seeing the inner and outer dimension is to cast valleys from smoke, to witness blue soil as weaving. What I say does not transfix, or ingest those strange electrical gusts which form inside inertia. All I can utter are classic visual diamonds, ultimately written by tumultuous aural mechanics. These are mechanics of depth, evolved from the pressure of unequal exposure. Seeming deafness, unequal balance, soaring hypostasis. I can only give you at this time preliminary auras, riddles, both free and irrational with exhaustion. I do not suggest that you fixate at this level. I do not ask that you persevere by testing your maturations by sounds which extend from mating leopards or gryphons. You be the judge, you are the ones who are now prone and a-priori. I'll know this when you'll begin to speak by a scattered and unseasoned phrasing. This is not to critique you, or make patterns from your strengths from what an old pronouncement has been. Certainly you are not crops, you are not something to be measured according to pylons or codeine. So if I betray any method it is to let the Earth's Sun live splayed before its first coagulation. It is to solemnly understand the forces which both bewitch us and betray us, according to the doors that we build which open and close according to randomity. And I think you understand that these initial talks are anterior to the solidification of species on the terrestrial plane. I have erupted as Mirach, as auto-poltergeist from Mirach. As Mirach, I remain partially inchoate, at one level audacious and trembling, at another, specifically pointed as astral magnification. Since the storms I provoke being leonine, they are both proto to this plane, and proto to this are planes conducted on Earth as though I exist as a verbal obeah doctor. The voice in this instance is an art which lingers by spells, by nigrescence as ominous allurement. So each vocal causation will tend to haunt, and re-gather, and re-specify. And in this haunting, in this re-specification, I'll gather a contingent of luminous bodies from Sirius gathering on Earth a superior osmotics filtering through English as their provisional glossematics. As this triple insemination we will infuse these moments of filtering over and beyond entropy guided as it is by suggestive demise. Remember, I am not catechizing you, I am only bringing to bear the in-exhaustive visibilities which state themselves by non-appearance.

As you become conversant with the Earth, with its panthers, with its artists, you understand, like a Yoruba enveined inside his antelopes, the precocious results kindled by the void through ferocious inclusionary status. I too am invisible to these 3-brained beings* which Gurdjieff imagined on Earth, with their sources of pottery, with their condoned tribal entanglements. At this stage of their existing they have not been prosperous. A certain element of their kind has overtaken them and poisoned them, so now they are forced to immerse themselves in the Northern interpretation of matter. We will begin to speak through our existence to save them, to enact for them new imminence and grace procuring for them an identity, so that new forces can become engaged, by transmuting glyphs according to energy that spins as trans-rational embodiment.

Mirach: Strategic Electrifications Part II

You do not reflect or absorb, you remain at this time hidden from the Sun. Of course this is a proto-strategy which allows your sands to linger proto to fulguration. Because to linger allows principles to erupt, to evolve a land of magnetism, combining your powers of radiance through the force of indexical signets.

I introduce, I lay the groundwork, I introduce you to stunning sums and complications. Again, I'm bringing forth complexity from the inchoate, from an orography which listens, which traces infernos by opening up tremendums. I know that you are susurous with the void, that you exist as interactive itinerants, always roaming throughout vertiginous potentia. I am only preparing you for a momentary foray inside earth, with its molecules according to irregular limitation. I repeat, we are not saviours, we are not those visible bodies grossly invigorated by atomics. I am not fictitious or populous in that I convince a billion or more beings to conduct themselves as if continuing to live by means of the agony of a body on a cross. Because we hear, because we do not condone matter as the one single substance, we cannot, and will not, condone ourselves by the impaction of scripture, by projection of lateral dogma as ferment. A syllabus of in-velocity which recalls in its doctrines a syllabus by gangrene.

Of course there are books which exist concerning the one central saviour, concerning his contradictory mimetics which I see as evolving no further than official disrepute. Yet these books persist as a kind of carking magma, as an addictive kind of agency which infects by insidious ridicule. But, I am getting ahead of myself. As you settle

24

into breathing the lectures I ignite, they will take as their labialization, a current, a morphophoneme, which traces its origins back to the articulatory form that created human perambulation.

Mirach: Strategic Electrifications Part III

We've come to this plane suddenly amplified as matter, as an ark of moths listening within ourselves to the uninhabited as possibility. We've come to this present gyral fragmentation, to this bilious gyral colony, with its Saturns and its fragments, with its simulated ice, with its failed response on Europa. As to Earth and its inhabitants, they are shaken, the moon goes blank at certain hours, the Sun stammers, seasons reverse and tragically implode. I call the Earth the linchpin of the colony, where audition at its height can communicate with splendour. I am not here to assign you ports, or continents, or adjustment of continents, but to listen inside the maze of human mass transmission. Because we know in our hearing that it apocalyptically ails, that its current motives blister, that stagnation has set in. We cannot sanction its old morals, its stunned motives. But it cannot be prefigured according to hyper-physical anagogics. We cannot give them nouns and ask that they pray to these nouns. Therefore no codes exist, no charismatic iridium eras, allowing them to provoke a previous mode of exhaustion. This being a complex interior commencement ablaze at this sudden riddling juncture. At this fortification of loss, where the males are always poised to attack, armoured in regressive surcoats, and the women, taught to gather wool and water, creating dazed and insensate offspring. From what I can gather all their governments are mishandled, empowered by collective bribery.

So I've come to you to provoke the bones of introduction, to find in the present condition an electroaffinity for translucence. A life where glass burns, where motives imply a fructifying cipher. Even now we affect the plane according to the sounds which now blaze from their originating idols. The Nilotic pantheon is now speaking, not in terms of their prior hieroglyphics, but in terms of the way that a boulder utters noise, or the way that a scorpion utters orchestration to the moon. Sounds to which canyons respond, by which a proto interiority is brought forth. This is the beginning of intense connecting fevers. Therefore, for want of a better term, we are great connecting spores, aligned with sounds that burn as life through interior justification. I've mentioned the conflicted princes of poetic reportage and carnage. Homer, and Virgil, and Dante. Instead of punishing armies and conflict I know we prefer winds which fly across the Sun, of light-year intaglios exploding from the myth of mountains. No, not the pneuma of being as cold phenomena by action, but as life through true confabulation and power. And I mean, not energy captured from exploded ducts, or that blazes as empty paradox, but ascent through the flames of a greenish vertical tree. In this sense I can speak to all of you here and not here. Of you from the zones of Altair, of you from the auras of Bellatrix, of you ignited by spells from Antares. Knowing that we have sprung from intrinsic vacuity, not transparency by scale, but transparency as witness which interprets itself to itself, so as to vary itself as solipsistic fury. This being poetic as fire, as thirst, as dialectical herrings inside clouds. This latter partaking of volcanoes and water, though you, such as Altair possesses no volcanoes or water. At this juncture I cannot speak of Antares or of any of its diacritical sums which glance from its verbal documents and return to these documents creating in its wake a legendary fire through emotional concealment. Not a realia condensed as perfect leverage, but a zone which equates with the igniferous as voyage.

We have not come to Earth to make mockery of its corpses, or to create an anarchic sigil which terminates the species according to our personal condescension. No. What we've come to inspire is the simultaneous boundary, of life before and after death so that there is no difference, so what will begin to transpire in the race will be an insular levitation. The race will inspire paradoxical appellations, thereby roaming in a hyperbolic state, transcendental with hypertypography. I call this the basic gift of the heavens not strictly content with astronomical fraction. I call this the states of rawest purity, the interior tenor of each phoneme, with its inbred force, with its scopic torrents through zeniths. So if I say phantasmic animus, blackened mountainous ray, the words exist only to reveal and suggest. What I say is not contrived from a false concussive, or become rote or pablum as companionship to damage.

Never prone to the weathers as they are sparked on this plane, we will rise as electrical liberty, as advanced elliptical proto-duration, creating entry and re-entry as blankness which evolved through resistance. In this sense we align with thought practitioners in Nepal, aligning with the customs of phantoms. So as to broach the divisible which inspires the divisible. Again, we are both dark and night to the humans, we are the collective phase of penetrant skiagraphy. Soon we will speak as beings, as belletrists who ignite through rhythm the sorcerous Saturnalia of verbs.

Mirach: Strategic Electrifications Part IV

Why do suns blaze? Of course this remains a rhetorical transfinite. One can speak of central hydrogen combustion, of talismanic nuclear tracings, but of course this does not embrace the transcendent condition of a roving meta-osmotics. Because we roam in this vicinity of the cosmos we have transmuted scale through witness, our power evinced through conspectus as distance. A relativity which rotates, which implies the blinding gulfs, emitted from the irony of origin. I could call each sun a castle of squalls, or a sound which transposes germinated concussion. In this regard I can say that we are suns who have evolved as a choreography of phantoms, knowing that we commune through magnetic ambrosia. We do not exist in order to feed a prone psychology, or to feast our scars through tactile replication. We burn by created being. We burn by fractal as genesis. I can say that we spin as magnificent proto-phenomena.

So what am I revealing? A sudden access of facts damaged by mischronicled illusion? Or am I postulating difference fused at its core by broken devolvement?

I say to you, that none of this constrains by social lore or assessment. This by no means is structured by cognomen, or advanced theatrics opening the spectrum to a treacherous form of kinetics. No, we are other planes existing as private transparencies. Is it possible to say, unfractionated figments, perhaps, boiling cinder lagoons. What I can say is that the absolute Sun is alive, that its mode or absolute is not a static transfixture. This is not thought derived from plagiaristic contestation. I am speaking of the Sun of suns which makes of our light immortal transparence. Therefore, we enter other galaxies through mazes, and then the Sun of suns creates from its creation diverse drafts of the void. Through us, this registers as rays through intestinal saffron, dialectically transgressed through haunted polar flares in schism. Because we must appear to the Earth as haunted tribal sparrows, only because our tenseness derives from contentious solar ingemination. Therefore we evince a rhythmos, a prolifics, an aleatoric atomization, transcending number by law, or motif, or scribe. I mean by such transcendence skills neither struck nor elided by combustion. Some would say that we speak through dualistic alternation, through the way that a mean varies according to pestilence which transfigures planes.

We know that humans feed from darkness. That their histories approach necrosis, that treason can no longer contest or sustain them. Therefore, they have become sublime by derogation, with all action being allowed through cremated sensitivity. Maybe, we'll create an alphabetics through sound from smoky Hottentot parabolas. Not their present contentions based upon solidified aggression, but the bringing forth of a palpable mnemonics before the fires of the early cosmos was struck. I'm speaking of other contours, of other kelvins, of other concussive havens, over and above that which emits itself as the night. Which implies other micro-stabilizations. And you know, being as suns from other suns that language pre-exists the cosmos and all the numberless kelvins of the cosmos, being the motion of a dimless claritas. Of course this exists far beyond the altered implosion in lepers, or smokeless astragal conclusives, as something which cannot be stressed through Buddha, Epimeniades,* or Confucius. Let me say, the fertility of burning onyx as restoration. Perhaps the chimeric of philosophical sigils. Perhaps the darkness of water in oriental winters. Or perhaps a north being alive and heraldic with diamonds. Then I can say the east and flooding, and living green lions. Let me say, I will phonetically concur on certain names of the poets, though as a citizen from space I am barely cognizant with appellations, yet I am approaching their storms through primal internality as weight. This is known through the self as perfection through damage, through primal sociology as flaw. Thus, fertility announces itself as ink, condoned as a skeletal substance emitted from skuas. Thus, I've come to the sigil as impregnation by exhaustion being double aspects of itself. Perhaps we can enter into this zone of life as a many-headed dragon which even at a minimal mean mimics Cambodia and Persia. I have known and existed as explosion in the reeds, I have known the restoration of lightning in the limbs. In this regard I have translated bullocks, I have transcended through my cells' immaculate refulgence. This being flight which announces its condition through indexical codex. Thus, I am never solely beset by solemn intrications, which seem suspended in the mind according to wrath advanced by vehicular doubling. Such fate remains non-binding, never being prone to fractious locusts or morals.

As we further descend into the bodies which inhabit bodies, I will attempt to enunciate names and forms as they appear in the chronicles which condense and sustain themselves as judgement.

Mirach: Strategic Electrifications Part V

It seems we will inscribe stupendous drafting powders within the ark of numinous grounding dimensions. Humans have convinced themselves that the galaxies are distant, that their home Sun is proof of the non-existence of the in-judgemental as ambrosia, that have no powers to internally transcribe the infinite. Thus, they remain scrambled inside the zodiac stunted by fossorial aggression. We will look at the way their language works and prescribe a glow in the way that phonemes are charged, in that the verbs come to bear as symbology. Their language will spin over and beyond a cryptographic geometry, opening onto a level which I can call nothing other than a mutational osmology. A realm where localized mirrors are continuous, leaping to a level of magnetized liquifaction. Words on one hand will transcribe themselves through stellar tornadoes, and at another level mine from themselves a series of black sparks from other centigrades and spectrums.

We will start by inscribing in toneless ghost memorials, in unintended secrets which soar. Not scripted according to dazzling or ornamental contest, but as solar grail, as mode which lives through proliferous interior optometry. This being the essence of the Sun which ignites by the aromatic, by beatific scale which possesses oceanics. You have in your proto-presence powers to know this, which instills as cosmic mean the expectational, the bell as paradise allowing scopic pause through riddles. For now, there is a poet we will recognize called in the chronicles Pessoa.* Pessoa who advanced name after name, and name through embodied name. So there was continuous disembodiment, there was heteronymic genius escaping from cold and defended cellular hulls. This is someone advanced through mutational invention. Creation, as unintentional manganese, as elixir from secretive hydrogen plums, rife with solemn fructifying blizzards whose uncanny occlusions arise from obscure options burning with ideas which collapse and re-arise from cadavers. This being nothing other than an occulted zeal floating as wisdom from impermanent assault. It is life which ignites beyond the collective through suggestion, the latter claiming as reason the in-illuminant body. And by in-illuminate I mean the bleak understanding of dying as one's inevitable craft.

As for us, there exist no pre-claimed intentions, no belief, no tantamount phantasmagoria as pertains to limit which proclaims phenomena as eclipsed by the impossible. What we understand of Pessoa is that he existed as a code, as a spark, by anonymous referent. Because we exist as a triple or extended vertical anatomy, the agreed-upon human lifespan will vanish and transmute to incalculable duration. The sunken skulls, the teeth which decline with activity will tend to reverse their implosions, will tend to mesmerize their afflictions and re-appear as rotation on the other side of entropy.

Saying such, we will have helped the human to a vaster scale, we will have amplified futurity, then the complexity known by the gravitas in different heavens will continue to de-ramify its old inventions so as to seduce by this motion life through inexplicable kelvins. Kelvins, which exist by unknown tinctures, by forms which elevate beyond lower bodies which form through elevated drizzling. And these drizzlings are of atomic concerns which we'll examine in our sculpting of hydroxyl, in the energy of our in-culminate writings as we prepare the way for an unknown prairie as quanta.

Mirach: Strategic Electrifications Part VI

Should our presence have arrived between great meteor strikes on Earth, we would have roamed as vapour through blinding gargantua. The great lizards were dominant. Allosaurus, the ferocious Rex, the smaller swifter Deinonychus. We could discuss non-human priority, with its curious resolve, with its attempt at life through tabulation. None of its great creations would exist, the writing of pre-Kemit, nor the burial mountains which rise above the Nile. Each night would burn and summon a swarming post-existence. Then the swamps would unfetter our motion.

Never the voice stunted with trained diphthongs, with attempts at conservative dis-harmonia, so we come to Old English, to Beowulf, to Dante, to energy which dissolves heavenly thought transference. A carnivorous electrical dimension. One that equates with the mystery of sadness. We enter the first unhappiness of the carcass, this being the seismic zone of the ungenerous. And why do I state this as law, as a principle first thesis, because they have largely ceased to perfectly hear the invisible. I mean those who can perfectly call the preeminent. Yet, the latter power exists in the respiration which erupts from the translucence we call the Dogon people. They live in the depths, of sentience as crystallization. They, who renew themselves through mystical triangulation, through the solar food of fire and air.

Now my eyes squint and I see a poet in Spain named Alberti.* He evinces words on paper as if filtering salt from Pasqualis Martinez.* And my eyes squint again, and I see a man who once walked on this earth and spoke by eruptive guidance. I think his appellation was Breton.

Then I see an electrical nemesis in his liver, and the appellation in this liver seems to suggest a rivalry with a one named Antonin Artaud. Not a litigious order mind you, but lists which sporadically occur without conscious invective. Lists, over and beyond those residues brought by perception.

As I am random by occurrence and in-occurence, I am at times uncannily specific. By calling on the obscure, I tend to re-demography its oneiric leanings according to the substance of its aleatoric tenets. The latter alludes to the interior exploration of what I'll call my Nilotic waters. From this point I'll vanish and come closer and closer to the abstruse magnifications as they once took focus in the minds of great mystical cadavers.

Mirach: Strategic Electrifications Part VII

These are rays on black paper. Each utterance that I make are rays on black paper. Conundrums, multiples, half-wroughts. I refer to intrinsic incompleteness, to my proto-understanding of human depth through incompleteness. Such arrested application has become a planetary kingdom where the rays of which I speak become distorted by occultation. Not an occult, mind you, which deepens, which creates new energetics of vision, no, this is an occult which distorts the human plaintiffs with laws through which they self-distort themselves, binding their reactions so that they now peruse the cosmos by means of inverted blankness. Thus my audition instructs and points me to the fact of their unending cipherization, with the majority of the populace condoned by calamity. Thus, this is a kingdom imploding at the brink of the Sun, its peoples plagued by solipsistic misnomer, by tense equational expirations, with earthquakes and warfare, and saviours befouled by collusion. This remains the general condition. The body at risk, the collective conception putrescible with tribulation.

Of course we have not come to this plane to sow stones for a prone or ungracious discipleship, but to open the being to subtle solar ingestion, to spark through bodiless fervour thoughts which flow as riverine in-semantics. Thus, we speak to the mind which comports itself beyond critical largesse, compressed at another origin according to crucial largesse, compressed at another origin according to crucial and unbalanced ascent. Yet what we witness in the species are quarrels like the drone of uprooted lizards. Therefore, the collective conception as we know it seems indefatigable with fractiousness as stratagem. A blinding dossier as schism. Of course, we remain alien to these schisms and the ilk which seeks to outlast itself through acts of dysfunctional quandary. As if a hurricane were split by monological degradation. Therefore we exist as none of the policies of the above.

Again, we are rays, over and beyond the powers in a darkened generating gnome. And we know by focus of strength that the populations discussed have reduced themselves to cinder. In consequence there exists this general ash, this threatening dissipation held in coma by darkened civil authority.

Have we come to circumvent the tumult, to offer salvation to those ensconced by profane hypnosis?

Have we leapt the cometary belts only to keep the general populace hovering in the haunts of its former contact with matter?

Have we come to lecture and de-commodify abstract infinity?

What I can say is that all prior praxis is broken, the prior infidelity to being has been shaken. By the latter I am speaking of exteriorised monotony implanted in the psyche by Greek tribunals and systems. They, the masters of fragmental myopia, of disestablished waking estranged from the burning Sun. Athens, Sparta, Corinth, all missing from the Sun. What follows, is the Peloponnesian debit having toned the present conception so that it leans to the exterior and brutality by attainment. Thus, an electrics through transverse thinking. This, to us, the blazeless design, the mind which descends to inverse monomials. Humanity thus exists according to object, to quantification as binding, with no "superior power or purpose beyond man." These are lessons we can chart as essence by mundane destruction.

So what does the mentality un-glorify, or create through priority as mayhem? It seems to be the superior as priority, the substance which rotates beyond collective debility. This being the level maintained according to fire, according to that which exists through aboriginal candesence. This is true electrical germination, full of mongoose welters, full of eagles with burning talons. This remains our basic current, to hear the electrical within, to withdraw to the bottoms, to suddenly rise and encompass realms. Not an abstract encompassing conditioned by a retrogressive parlance, but evolved by radiance, by antispecious blinding, by charismatic psychic vitrescence, blowing away what the profane would conspire against us, they who attempt to seal us in old burial jars, while letting their brethren mock us for fleeting pecuniary gain.

We exist, not as unfoldings by mirage, or flameless sacrifice patterns, but as that which advances by sound through collective simultaneity. What is meant by sound is its essence as permeable realia. In solar worlds, in voids, sound ignites, existence burns. This is not light which constricts and measures the physical. Bodies no longer cohere at this level. This is why we can never generate form by means of concrete physiology. I stress and I must stress again, we are not saviours promoting behaviour from a latitude of morals. We've not come to display ourselves as a special miracle of ghosts. We are not a single power promising nations. In saying such we are not enacting a divided society, since we've taken up the seed of life on this plane, knowing as we know that the seed exists as inclusionary rotation. From what we can gather the Greeks took this seed and altered its rotation according to fragmentary process. Which in turn inspired a principle rationality which has now disfigured itself in the guise of collective paranoia. Thought at this level can never increase itself within the power of invisible seismology. By contrast, Nubians experienced the seed as fully rotational, for them, even the void was a gyral galaxy, everything was stored. Which in the deepest degree opened the way for collective transcendence in that the soul and the body were oblivious to chaos. The soul was not foreign to the animal as body, in this sense, simulacra does not arise until the governance of the Ptolemies. With the living seed in constant rotation certain scribes could weigh the rings of Saturn, or clarify planes within decibels of sodium. All knowledges possessed the visible and invisible as dialectic. Which naturally corresponds to nature in its collective gnosis. In this sense we mingle Nubia in our carbons, we experience the soils for salubrious strata of nitrogen, we transmute the cyclonic in order to suggest its aboriginal instigation. Because we've organically arrived to assist the Sun and its populations to restore the grace of their original spinning. Of course we are not tautology by square, nor cunning viral saturation quantified as topos by isolate figment.

Having balanced the excruciate by water we've come to know how mathematics builds itself in service of regression, how numbers ignite revengeful propaganda, so that certain lands and beings are demonized as fauna, having their wealth absconded and sailed across post-mortem waters. And now these waters across the planet have taken on the character of the liquifous as desert. With the kelp dying, and the latter-day Olmecs being subject to forensic opthamological incarceration, all the strategies for existing have become obscured. We having the power of unalterable nutation have gained lessons from dearth, have seen within reactive massacre a measure of salt, alchemically invigorated as transfigured mass. We are not speaking of salt as self-obliterated function, but of its delicate flaws which resist a monochromatic dimensionality. Which means we are open to what exists, also to what pre- and post-exists. Which is called in universal parlance, sphinxian, argot, impenetrable riddling. Under the law of prevailing matter it lives as transfunctional deficit, as non-occurring principle, always subject to general negation. Because we see the blind against the blind who kill through intrinsic drama, we inspire the present circumstance beyond endurance or indifference, having come to the human plane not prone to simplified decoding, but something other than engendering a didactic truth. Therefore we will work as a fulminate scattering hive. Again, it is not a work proclaimed as dis-invention where the scope of reason is invoked to procure inclement social honing. Our concern ultimately rests with the Sun. Their Sun, the human Sun, the Sun of the continents, which repeats dawn after dawn, everyday as their Sun. Because we hear at such a level we can invoke a cellular state in their Sun. By invoking enigma through resurrection we cleanse the field of its rotation, allowing new rays to come forth as metamorphic penetration that advance beyond a tortured conquering mission, gaining from our power refundment from a divisive psychical scale, by advancing evolved philosophical torrents.

The leaders of their lands continue their slaughters by darkened motifs, by stringent variations, always seeking triumph by matter, by aggrandized simulacra as profit. There is nothing left to propagate at such a level. This is why we hear by nutation, by invisible orality, understanding human psychic germination in terms of a neural or stellar fissioning. I mean the neural and the stellar as simultaneous waves.

Not insidious corrosion as passed through the degrading modes of dialectial confinement. Again, nutation, and the evolution in the genes of an organic electrical environment. Certainly, not an army firing guns at the heart of a cyclone, but something inordinately more mysterious than a treatise on owls. Such a treatise evinces a certain ocular display, but at another depth it leads back to the specific instigation which fuels uncountable stellar arrangements. In this regard we are silent, we are a peculiar system of cycles existing on Earth as random nutation. No, our source remains the uncanny, and we, the interlocutors of the uncanny. We are not here to quell by monocentrism the divided spoils of warring populations, or didactically address the disease of universal distraction. We understand that there are needs of a divided populace, of a chronic populace crippled at the core by paradigms of certain xanthrochroids.

Our light spins as both steam and transparence without the pattern of chronos as template. So if we sum up the Greeks as xanthrochroids this is certainly not a hollow or nefarious summalia. Being is thus effected by nutation, not in terms of a forest of tumbled arctic waves, but in allowing the mind to flow as transparency, to see through the sorcery of tangled apparitions. One could say that I speak by means of notable irony, creating by my tone a scarcity of minerals, a sparse totemic overtone, thereby complexifying trust. This is what I'll call delimited embrasure, broken modelling as noir. So it is in this state that I'll speak of the principle saviour of this era. For instance, the sky goes mute when signaling his astrological specifics. So is the Christos, void, a misnomer in strange context, a Doppelganger, a cosmological carpenter falsely bred through insufficiency? Prejudicial arc, miscarried power? Let me stress, this is not a doctrinal overview, but a seeping agitation as expressed by the Sun. We are not seeking a message of wolves, or creating spartan quotas in a virtual battle garret. This is neither our cause, nor our mission. We have come to ease human neural regression. We are not as saviours who have appeared from non-existence, that we have been carved from bluish lightning, so as to signal an epoch under the auspices of a Roman city. But if we scroll through schematic dates we will alight upon the Kemetic chapter. The urge of resurrection appeared within the Kemetic condition circa 10,000 B.C. This being the lunar God Osiris which predated Judea, and the extenuating circumstance of the Christos before the likes of Pontius Pilate. Yet we are not enveloped in dark emotional confiscation. What I speak of is a script which ignites from intuitive cinder. Again, Osiris emerges. His magical rise, his abbreviated life, his scattering in pieces. Again, we do not stress any biased maniacality, or any doubtful apperception. There exists no blinding, no undue recitation concerning the Christos, and this widely known Biblical deficit. Because we are not seeking a guide who casts light on the powers after death. In this sense we have no leanings towards a legendary mourning. What I've said are nothing more than telepathic bursts, nothing more than unraveled sonar. Let me say that if one were searching for a perfect stellar oasis it would exist in the wake of a Nilotic Isis, faithful mother, goddess of grain and corn, "Nurturer," "protector," according to forgone annunciation of the perfect light from Osiris. According to this tenor a greenish stellar locale being nothing less than the simultaneous interiority which alchemically confounds probity which is operant from the focus of transverse expertise. In terms of eminent magnification we can speak of the Earth's equator as a primal mystical salt being infinity through human grasp as extension. This allows me to say that there extends a certain grace on Earth, which transmixes itself and becomes a horizontal zenith.

We, the apparent volatility, the sigil which proclaims our writing as the misuse of ghosts, as patternless aortas, as uncritical wailing. We are none of these missions, none of these tenacious criticas. Again, the sigil as light from misspent microbes. Because priority exists in terms of mundane balance, power appears to re-translate its options through the force which projects from a segmented lion. So if I project myself through a body seeing how visibility inheres, I could adapt or dignify a singular camphor by which its living parts strengthen or weaken. I cannot think by means of superficial lessening creating from such a summons emblems from a runic sortie, but because of rational adumbration there now exists misaligned ascent always making war on the inseparable. And what accrues is inconclusive judgement. Which has resulted in a monarch of false bodies. And I mean by this monarch the leaders we squint to see through the lenses of the sea. Each one of them advanced through flailing technical tribulation stunted by powerless constitutional revelation. Unlike the ethers we inscribe there exist no transparent sun fields through law, through pointless discourse on weaponry. Perhaps we'll imply ourselves as Buddhists in Goa,* or perhaps as scribes in the night fields of Mali, giving to Sirius perfect assonance through darkness, bringing forth its lesser harmonic as mathematic compadre. For instance, we will know its power to resurrect itself from fractionated glyphs so as to be at one with our understanding over and beyond the present Sun sometimes darkened through in-commissioned respiration. Of course this is to listen to light thereby allowing the Sun as the maker of all strengths to leap beyond the fatality of outcome, which again will allow it grasp of translunar civilization.

The xanthrochroids have stated that the invisible can exist as no proper continuum, that its thunders are as beasts, vague, that none of its majesties can proceed. This being the paradigm being presently applied to human formulation. There remains a reliance on plain spoken boast, on plagiarized meta-positions. Let us take the age of Pericles, it is a subsequent era, not because of any lack of intrinsic magnificence, but because its grasp of inner darkening was poor. As one Naim Akbar* has observed, life within this realm, always constrained to observable activity, its life and consciousness being identical with physical process. Such thinking subsists upon the assumption of the body as abstracted burning, as having no more than a visible group of implements in order to build and destroy. Again, I am not insisting on negatives, on lost and un-crystallized anagrams. Yet I contrast Athens with transmutive stellar nutation, with cellular renewal and the rising of the dead. I ask again, how can such thinking exist by nutation, how can it attest to a greater outcome other than victory through war?

I, Mirach, am not supercilious with anguish, or constantly rekindled by despair. None of this forms me through acts of petrification. The agon has never taken root and does not apply. My light is not etched by misnomered fuel. There I am not the Mirach condoned through measurable distance. By droning I quietly hound the mind bringing forth elements which constantly questions its own repulsions. These are elements which announce themselves through focus throws, through parallel idioglossias. This is why whole leaven seems to distort by giving itself gestures, not unlike a Kemetic mandrake root always ascending, always taking on intuitive spectres as unquenchable doubles. Which is so unlike the taking of steps measured time after time by exoteric metier. What I speak of is not the failure of a worrisome contest, or pursuit constrained according to a formless mass in an athletic ray. So when I argue against constraint it remains the blocked ascendance which withdraws itself into world after world after world. Which means the freeness of our gain is like a glance which ascends through blue roses. And this is not a critique or simple praise in order to provoke a compensatory flaw, or re-invigorate in its wake a mishandled ambrosia. Because we are not here to condone or reformulate the human as an embattled or repetitious mystique. Again, nutation. The provoking of drought within the absence of drought so as to re-ascend the sigil, which takes its means not only from waking mirage, but from a depth which creates ascent from a poisonous core. Not an umbilical luxury, or a supercilious social comradery, but a kind of mental vaporization which comes to experience the source of its trance. Not a simple choreodrama, but an investigative symbol unrelated to scarcity of the triumph of reason.

I'm speaking here of protracted energy where the cells instruct themselves much in the manner of an evolutive whirling. I call this an outcome where saffron ignites and causes to accrue an aboriginal fertility, where one responds to nature as given, thereby mutating the visible through the invisible thereby merging with sound which extends through numeric cipher. If one could plot a direction it would be north of the great balance, higher than the fulcrum ledge, the body then becoming a luminous geo-turbulence, a fount within a maturating spectrum. This is not the square of dice by enigmatic tumbling, but the micro-self in earnest listening to its own eruption through anonymous mystical perseverance. Such a course is not derived from annulled ideas as a separable beast. We instinctively understand as such all of us belonging to the same inscrutable foundation. We are suns as delimited wholes feeding ourselves from a glossary of diamonds. We who subsist beyond draconian fatigue, beyond a humanistic drainage where strain is compounded by a dossier of ash.

I'll call the higher level infectious blue carbon, intuitive exploritics where a fundament of atoms is unleashed. This being the primordium as mantra, the unblended scale, not unlike the tide or the drone which responds from an inclement meteor. This remains the scroll as quanta, as unwhitened list, as observational in-suggestion. At this removal there remains no blood to suggest us, no flock of accessible remnants extracted, say, from a dampened crocodile in its lair.

Because we exist as powers of interior nutation, we spawn growth through ambulatives, as pensive ozonal implication. This is how the neural state invigorates, and evolves through electrical misnomer. For instance, during certain dawns, we arise in the blood of Bangkok, at hounded margins threatened by erasure. In this regard, we resemble the confines of Niger, with its wanderings, with its camels a-lit by turbulent inner terrain. And this is not collapse or erosion by central bonfire or exhibit, but a rhetoric advanced as a porous and calamitous hydroxyl.

So I ask, should the human race be spat upon as flaw, as hounding specification? Should its impact remain winnowed by liminal political osmosis? Perhaps humanity in its present tenor could be christened as convulsive geriatrics, or perhaps its drama could be termed a nightmare mislaid in the sands. Its recent manifestation has been a reactive solar inversion which has resulted in an isolate cognitive deficiency, this being a collective spell resulting in tragic hypnotical concurrence.

But let us examine the source of its Memphatic tables, its stellar source compounded in the Nile. I know we concur with such understanding as we see life manifested by Osirian example, by his circular operation within various psychic Nomes. In this regard we can speak of the human form as resurrected cinder, as isomorphic infinity. Not conduct by flameless battle, or a body in a faceless palace prompted by maintenance of a pointless instruction. According to Osirian insurrection humans are connected by altimeter flame, by interactive voltage. These remain the trace rebellions in the human secret, the disestablished law, the assembled heat, the nucleic timing. The result of this trace magnetics is now a susurrant physiology become an involuntary being who commences to utter in Algerian neutrino. Or maybe light from a quaking Nubian persona, electrically condensed, yet rising above a strange pollutional trellis. Life is then commenced above the transverse forces which are honed by common historical assessment. Life is no longer sought through the uni-directional as ailment, but as inverse baptismal by a blank mutative lightning. Perhaps a diagram which dissolves and elevates quintessence, or perhaps an arc which spans beyond the zodiac. Which creates inside my voice a potent gust of premonition. A mountainous or enriched concurrence as slag, which explodes the dust within its spinning viral chamber.

Again, we elect osmosis. Not that we are coding a complex secret, but that we have invaded beyond the known origination of the Earth and the source of its central Sun. We are primal factors in a compound lightning stroke, in a compound solar inculcation. Never a sterile reclamation of acres, or to a claiming of cults by belief in a central traumatizing leader enthralled in the fire of veniferous paradigms. Not the vocables of the current zodiac, be it taurean, or ram, or fish. Nor is it the traps in haunted schist analogous to carious occlusions within neurology. Never are we mirrors or faceless gladiolas in the face of such struggle emptied by an in-coming bleeding. We understand the aforementioned leadership as graft by metastasized destruction, by poison as corroded industry. This, the human bickering within a frayed internal land which burns. Thus, an atrophy fraught by perturbation. This is what can be called a suffocated matrix, a mantra schismatic with lucre.

Here we are in this blue inevitable scriptorium never plotting against the Sun, but understanding its cosmology of application with its shifts, with its enigmatic day grafts, spinning in union with the text of local stellar debris. Let me say, that the Sun has proclaimed a momentary lessening, a classic in-reunion with itself, like leaves on a magnificent starvational tree. Its loss of dialectical spotting is symbolic of a lack of its previous respirational health. Which results in dazed projections which results in collective neural in-direction. Which has become the blind intent of light, poisoned in the sense that it enhances the state where collective carnage rises to intolerable acuity. If the race has become fearlessly Osirian in demeanour it could begin to parse depths and pieces of chaos and meld them in concert and then extract its leaven from the hypnotic trepidation of the blood fort. As energy other than theistic crusaders we do not allow such swamps to claim us by conveying interior torpor ministered by mythological unease. In this regard our marrow is inviolable, is never prone to the variation which seeks a simple succour from quelling and re-naming the didactic.

Thus depths transpire in the auditory field, and by audition an optical neurology begins to self-invoke as a crystalline advantage with an endless sea of trees. This is the plane of great suffusional suggestion which osmotically seeps through the human species as pure nutational poise. It is like seeing the Sun slowly rise from a furtive plain of salt. Salt being the body as elemental beacon, as we, through intuitional randomness witness kindled individuals awake as psychic spirits even as their bodies continue to panic at a furious depth of transmixture. Between the visible and the invisible, between the kinetic body and thirst nomadic palingenesis roams through Mali and Niger, and the Hopi lands to the west. By understanding the flames of their higher nitrogen farming, both life and death newly rise to transmute themselves over and beyond a stunning obsolescence. Thus, the empire of mammon no longer applies. If, for instance, I took 30 beings from Venezuela, and prompted them according to medial accusation, none of them would reply in the defensive modes of an old protected boundary. From this it can be said that the model of individual placement has vanished. Metropolitan conjecture no longer persists. Life and death then fuse in tornadic Osirian, becoming the source of human molecular transfunction. Not the body as fixed, but free standing in being. So menial accusation can go no higher than the secondary plane ruthlessly invoked by Northern or pragmatic law. And it is because of these Northern principles that erosive schism persists, creating within the pureness of one's myth a bevy of penal clauses so that all maturation reduces itself to doubt. At best the mind becomes oblique, and subsists through irregular feelings according to a dominating pecuniary ire. Thus, absorption by the spirit becomes neutered, with the bio-invisible being scattered.

In this era which consumes us, the sun peoples suffer, always roaming through disadvantage, embroiled in basic quarrels with stark survival.

And we know this because we hear their interior phlogiston, their impecunious saturations, which paradoxically signal bio-electric elevation. But this latter condition seems to inspire brazen opposition in the northward leaning genes. Say, if we are absorptive and secret the extrinsic personality accuses and causes lingering defamation as was the case with the geographer d'Avezac,* when he accused the continent of Africa as being bereft, being consumed by what would be said in a modern sense, of being disabled by aphemia. The inability to utter words "due to emotion or psychoneurosis." He dismisses its inherent synesthesia, accusing the whole continent of not belonging "to the history of the development of human civilization." Such assessment seems to retain its status in the European substratum not so much as a discernible grain, but as a subtle psychic linkage. An energy which seeks curtailment of the Sun, which seeks to increase a world stymied by the ambush of products. Which becomes a transverse intensification which blinds, which distracts the energy of one's radix by means of puzzling components. All of these components being imminent with scattering, apply as their complexity evanescence commingled with proto-evanescence, which structures realia within forms of the inconsistent.

Our suffusion of Earth has obliquely shifted to those whose realia is Kolarian,* whose audition is bio-chemical with primordia. The body in such a state is not a stationary rock, nor is it cold with exacted sub-feeding, but it's an interactive glyph alive with nervous moaning. And this moaning is not sorrow, or civilized protraction by faith, but is the fire of exploration spreading from the cells, then wandering into language. Which brings to mind the dark consumptive test which is present in Dravidian. "The Indus Valley,"* Mohenjo-daro,* Harappa,* the mystery of the "Indus script."* All of this somehow buried within the current generational dimension, a dimension with its corruptible angst, with its tedious interrogations going no deeper than the frontal or exterior posture. For this dimension the non-observable is always empty, the transpersonality is always negated at its source by microscopic burden and the authorities of that burden. This paradigm, always condensed by observation, by bones constructed by biological chance. Such was not the life as the core of Mesopotamia, nor did such expression affect the dimensions of the soul as it crystallized "into an Eighth or Divinely permanent form." As divine example we find it flaring from the Nilotic peoples like invisible ions roaming aboriginal vistas. What I'm speaking of is not utopian, and remains unscathed even in the wake of modern cortical oppression. The latter we've come to know as a dark empirical weight filled by figures amassed by a superficial timeline. Say, if a human amasses a certain retention of time in his life he is required to posses a certain fraction of objects, to aspire to exorbitant dwellings, while inculcating values of this mean in the minds of various offspring. So within the family there never exists ritual advance but only count by dodecahedra. This is how the modern mental form is grown. Any change of scope is never emboldened, never embraced. Instead, the mind is encompassed on the one hand by ferocity of denial, and on the other by the opaque threat of post-terrestrial damnation. Because of this one is always seized by adherence to mechanical proof, to the ongoing testament of matter as the single expressive law of life, which naturally extends to technocracy and enterprise.

Do we wish for adherents, for the sacrifice of those who breathe inside our morals? What I can say is that we have not appeared as a bastion of priestly misnomer, nor do we contentiously adhere to any populist mephitic. Again, we have not succumbed to faulty lexical procedure, nor have we considered the assemblage of bodies as proof of our coherence. If this were the case we would present ourselves according to anthropomorphic vocable. The latter would be confined to the margins of normality, with any vocal gold emitted considered within the flight of porous metals. But again, we are not a seminar sustained within the obvious. I, Mirach, at riddling light year remove, at the pinnacle of capacious uranian form, a "Yellow-orange giant," linked to the powers of you, Bellatrix, of you, El Nath.

We are now transmuted in this blue scriptorium of feeling. We have invaded the Earth through hearing, with neoteric emblems which writhe inside a dark or voided condition. And this dark or voided condition remains as a collective adherence to the mineral as unit, to the impairment of the Sun roaming inside a tense symmetrical perspective. We are not here to politically unbind a dense monarchical door, or open up a framework where pointless strictures can cohere. We understand that the race which now assumes itself feels the pressure from its limited strata. They now rule themselves within the stunning disquiet of an unsettled nuclear province. For instance, if one flamelet goes bad the Earth will witness itself as massive expiration. A bereft extinction simply lost to itself as unrecoverable panic. Of course we have not designed this, or worked in terms of compiling assaultive lists. Of course we do not access this experience through dazed or uneven blinding. The collective carcass is clear; it cannot face its longevity. And we understand by longevity those aboriginal rejoinders no longer acknowledged as living. I call these rejoinders invisible sub-states, a-correctional equivalents which naturally empower all living generations. This is not war as envisioned by Virgil, but movement through in-canonical tracings. The subtle, the incantatory, the in-ballistic. As suns we are cast in shadow, as lions, we are sigils invisible in orbit. Therefore, we understand the loss of respiration in the oceans, we understand the humbling of all the species, for instance, the howl of the Costa Rican Puma,* the troubling reversion of the Key Largo Wood Rat. Let us be clear, we are not worshiping ruins, we are not concerned with re-invigorated exhaustion. This being the opposite of insolence. We being suns who insinuate energy as risk, always transmixed with a threatening termination, yet we risk the hazardous flaws which persist in the in-dominate. Thus, we cannot perceive through centralized dictation, as if attempting to dominate a flock of birds flying from centripetal Nigeria. These latter being beings who cosmically self-migrate, who transcend the poles, who amass their own dictations. Which impacts us with the flow of enigmatic interjacence, where the zodiac shifts from its current solar vortex and takes on an organic experiment where the proportional domain is no longer magnetic with the fumes which were cast from old reptilian transmission. Which also includes the domain of buildings, and roads, and thoughts as they currently persist. We are saying this as powers projected from the root of nebulas unrelated to a carking secondary source. And what is meant by secondary sources are forces misplaced by nostalgia, according to historic ruin, according to human effort manoeuvered by the dis-articulate.

This remains the locus of the xanthrochroids with their centrality condoned through hearsay, by re-created dis-remembering. And it seems this God, this centrality, condoned through hearsay, condemns the tenets which inhere at the source of the melanotic. It retains the

Rig-Veda in spirit with its castes, with its tenets, which denunciate the untouchables. Always the Brahmins with the more northern colour at the pinnacle of the castes, with the Dravidians consisting of the lowest positions given the task of providing the cleansing of unswept reptile salts. But we are listening for those who provide the cleansing of unswept reptile salts. We are listening for those who have stumbled beyond civilian incorporation, beyond the social deficits of law. They who now absent themselves from the dilemma which accrues from profit and money. They who float inside suffusional direction, ignored by the wrath accrued through metropolitan confusion. As if they ascended the inner stones on the wings of imaginary herons. Yet we are not here to propagate a particular racial technology but to understand the equation between suffusional light and essence. We understand by this the absorption of rays, and by extension an osmotic self a-symmetrical with essence. As to interior kinesis we can ignite within the confines of 815 B.C. and speak with a Doctor of Phoenician trading and pottery, of someone who listens to the metaphysics of sailing or silk as beauty. Who could command by such beauty the murex of Byblos,* and the wines of Iberia. Such a Phoenician is not the simple physique of minerals, or their employ conducted through precepts gained from the tribulation of monsters. What is spoken through this current is the osmotic circulation of interior solar transparency, which remains as far as we can see the isle of perfect concentration. And I mean by concentration those figurements in the being unbeknownst of themselves which recall the aforementioned suffusional being, soaked with aeration and soaring. We are speaking here of an internal collective, of wings and beings magnetized to eternity. Again, there is no flight by expected direction. Because we cannot breed exclusion we cannot say that all the elements in the North have bred lessening and disappearance. Let us recall Kierkegaard's neurasthenia and his conflict with the Danish church and its organizational grounding points. On first appearance he seems to be an isolate signal, of one who experienced the grace of the untoward. We can only say that in the subconscious havens nervous heat appears. We can speak of a Frenchman named Breton who absconded rigour in terms of its frontal disadvantage. His was an attempt of the North to reblend with the South, to again work with suffusional syllabi. We understand these adjustments, these powers, which awake by immaculate brewing. These are traces of the old original paradigm "to achieve...freedom from oneself." This being the gift which accrues from higher thinking. Thus, one becomes open to the fevers of telepathy, to spontaneous gatherings of sound which crystallize as astral gnomonics and grammar. Again, a curious suffusional dynamics. Not a bartering for ozone, but a language which tarries and elides, with each letter suffused by a hovering hydroxyl.

By use of such language one takes on what I'll call a positive contraction, then one begins to live as an an esoteric sub-species. A hidden practitioner in being, taking as one's power part absence from visibility. One becomes a navigable in-vicinity, a kinetic unvoidable substrate creating an interior climate not unlike medicinal residue from ether. Which creates a murmuring, a susurrant phonemic in the cells. An energy which leaps from the susurrant phonemic in the cells. An energy which leaps from the field of proto-integration, and becomes an anagram of breathing, with the latter taking as its aerographic a spellbinding rhythmos.

As to standardized application is this biological abnegation? Is this a sterile chimericality?

What is being spoken here, Khaba?* Akhu?* The soul as invisible biology?

The answer protracts itself in the affirmative, in galvanizing ponds which protract themselves as distance. The marrow transmographies, the body becomes an unseen flexibility capable of other planes and zones other than the palpable as criticality. Not that the palpable is discarded, but its dazzling semaphores of breakage are now seen as a zone of conduction reachable by expanded paths. And these expanded paths transmix with otherness, with a zone of respiration not tolerable as fragment. Such a body requires no wheat from glaciated farmlands, no recipes replete with decisive caloric enhancement. We are speaking of paths which fueled the nature of Piankhy,* which fueled the interior transfusives of King Necho,* circa 600 B.C. Which brings to refulgence the Khaba as "locomotion," as "omnipresence," with the Akhu being the fuel of dazzling mental genetics. This being the state of genetic roads above the ozone, of the immortal personality in seeming situ. And since the immortal personality partakes of the uncountable, the body with its vehicular motif transmutes and takes on Saturnian utility, takes on the premise of inverted lightning hills. Which weigh without scale, without substance which subsists as frontal projection. So what persists in the thinking is a constant flickering of solar flares, of old Egyptian double crowns, of sacred parasols, of beings of purplish stellar demeanour, which embodies the dimension we'll call Akashic* solar scrolls. And as these solar scrolls we simultaneously flow as a river of photinos. Of course this provokes another tenor of priority heard in the mind by means of a susurrant electrical scale. Sans religious scale, sans a despicable social scale. We as suns creating in our wake impalpable transhuman interiors. A salubrious stellar accomplishment whose powers are not claimed by judgement or terror. No. We are working with the living and the living dead. Certainly not the neo-empirical as occultation, as identifiably pragmatic condoned by exoteric transparence. We have reached the level of nuance as sea, as that which carries all the current beyond the galaxies. So that being who will newly persist will peer perhaps, from bereftness and war, from famine in some haunted or anonymous garret, thus, leaping out of history and the circumstance of evil. These are beings who absconded from devolving micro-achievements, from the wayward scrawl marks of techne. God being no more to them than cooked metal and glass. But the questions remain: have we entangled light? Have we superimposed new zodiacs?

It must be stated and stated again that the parent Sun is now ailing. During the hegemony of the xanthrochroids perilous psychic poisons have been bred and created static within its higher respiration. Because the Sun and the Earth breathe as one body, they exchange themselves through empathy. So when the dominant paradigm remains frontal, deeper aspects are lost and the sensitivity of transmission is corroded. We are speaking of a rapacious inner plight as regards the darker inhabitants who are closest to the Sun. Being that a cycle of the Sun has completed the power of mechanics is less dominant, technology wavers at the end of "Great Year,"* and opens at a remove beyond unrest. New unfoldings occur. It seems that the ground is giving way, thus, tornadoes burn, floodings ignite from the invisible. During the present interjacence no sequential apparatus seems to exist. Beings are living and dying within this realm of interjacence. But because of the interjacence, activity is compressed, what was once understood as the length of a consensus year has now collapsed to a volume of seconds.

Disorder rules, the individual being becomes instinctively prone to sudden tributary quakes. The blood rattles, the eyes go dim, the mind ceases to link itself to any linear record or outcome. So it is within this dimension that we as new suns apply alchemical suffusion and ray.

We supply a momentary compass full of directionless compost. What happens at this cusp is that rays appear in the void, rays, from El Nath, rays from Bellatrix, rays from the incoming Altair. True, other suns could have heard my call and come to assist the Sun in its allusive bout with congestion. This is not a tautology, or a ruse, or an indication condemned to chronic alluvial haunting. Not an errant futility, or a broken or metaphysical carpentry engulfed by numerical distance. To the human practitioner this is frightening, this is torture transmixed with the formless. But from another approach, this is the deficit of adventure, the curse which invades collective need for avoidance reaction. These are sums which react in the collective presence that includes the human myth with its boundaries and distortions. So what I say tends to convulse the subconscious lair by a lingering or pre-dominant panic. This is not life as simple botanical grain, but an open utilization which charges the energy field with strokes of balletic evolvement. Perhaps a burst in one, or boiling slumber in another. A compound molecular lattice which means the universe is never solved and is relentless with energy. Not something on the plane of Newtonian clockwork errata, not the clauses of itself bereft at its source by mere exterior arrangement, but the subliminal as mythology, as form by associational spell. Such spells condense as the free flow of energy through blank conduction in the being. Again, not a frontal charisma, not an open or accessible burning exposing a direction measuring by external leaning in the being. Here we speak of body as ghost, as multiple being in being.

An analogy on Earth would be what the Egyptians called the BA*
which linked the breath to the "spiritual soul," this being the blazing
ink in the upper spectral body. One then becomes kinetic with strange
subliminal salt, and from this a trans-connective begins to transpire so
that our rays begin to activate within the individual neurology, which
means reaction flares into another or acute ascending point, so that
the body becomes a conductor of destabilized alterity as current. At
one level the being is dazed by dint of alchemical trans-function. The
BA being of occulted blackness, and the Kha being the gold of the
BA, being the Sun as compounded solar emission. And what is meant
by compound is the compression of all stages, of all the subjoined by
cascaded response. The being then takes on the weather of a prone
alchemical property. He or she then conjoins with a voyage which
rows by the mathematics of voltage, all of one's motions becoming
micro-infinite in approach, becoming nuance after nuance on the
migrational scale, thus fusing with the electro-magnetics of carbon.
This is not a discriminatory haven where beings are horrifically cast
aside, where whole quantities are bred for extinction and the dousing
of memory. The latter is not the condition of our substance, nor the
energy which we emit through our suffusional spectrums. Again, not
a monochromatic leakage, or a monochromatic insight bred by one
colour. Instead, we roam in green omegas, always pouring suggestive
ions. Therefore we cannot exist as stark exclusionary samples akin
to suddenly condensed figures prosaically supping at a specific Polar
cafe. Saying this, I can never append to us heroic example as hubris, or
to carving microbial schist with our feats.

Within this post-summarization I can say that life can never be viewed from objective supposition, but as riddle, as sound at the borders of chaos, being sigil at seeming capacious incapacity. But what is meant by insufficiency? Do we cherish emblems so as to embellish case histories so as to create kinetic parallels through context? Or do we at some point eliminate mysterious elements to pointedly specify the human through sociology, by writhing, by enclosing condensed spectrums in an isolate colonnade? This is not the circumstance for issues and grammes which nervously mis-states. Thus, we remain as stark suffusional ether living inside the floodings of neurology, thereby understanding the thirst which rises from the molecules thereby finding the temperature which rises above old sequentials. If one hunts for meals, or works with hunting dogs or bison, the interior intelligence of which we speak creates a spiritual hieroglyphics of waking. Thus, our light maintains its seepage through the oneiric cascading of doubles. And these doubles are the infinite pantomimes in being. Again, they are psychic gusts which form increasing multiples of themselves. Of course these are not conscripted citizens that we are discussing, but beings who breathe by blank harmonia and vertigo. Alive as non-abstractions, they live through tumultuous spectra according to clarified audition.

Arbitrary?

Scale which ascends and descends according to the aleatoric?

Neither prevails as definitive or outright declaration as answer. The realia now discussed convenes at the level of a spectral tenor which represents the complex nature of spiraling secondary states. Which do not cohere as a meddlesome rowing, but an upward or Akashic translation. So, in this upward dimension parallels transfigure, octagons transmorph. The seeming physical scale is released and re-invaded by its own invisibility, thus, the living body becomes its own suffusion, becomes in fact simultaneous with suffusion.

So they are you, El Nath, as conundrum of spirals, they are you, Altair, who have surmounted their own resistance, Bellatrix they carry your auras, as for me, Mirach, they become blessed by my audition.

With the perfect ignition of fish, with the pluperfect sorcery of angles, I, Mirach, am both this sub and dominant tenor, which leans this way or that according to rotational glintings. And these rotational glintings being the transcendent commingling of human suffusional gatherings. Yet of these suffusional gatherings we cannot know them in terms of their lying side by side in a quantitative lair. Yet we feel their ethers trembling, their blindnesses transported to pervasive shimmering, so that suffusion transmixes and combines in a state of transmundane engulfment.

El Nath: On Huertas*

I do not come to speak in terms of greater disconcertion, to create terrifying epistles so as to isolate my spectrum and divert my own monstrosity to an approach which erupts through monocentric constriction. Therefore I summon all my electrical forces so as to bring all my genetic carbon to bear concerned as it is with Earthly nutation. In order to balance numbers and districts one must come to equate seismic mystification with what I'll call erupting conundrums. As El Nath, I have seen genetic distance across interstellar prolongation, and so crops blaze, new being is expressed, the summation of folly is then riven. But not through idealistic dialectics, mind you. Beings are like huertas, they grow through variable quanta. In an exomorphic sense they behave as mesmeric ornament. Constrictive quanta would suggest ginger, dates, certain oranges from Valencia. But because they express heat, their mirrors burn as decimals which implode inside soil. In these soils numbers react according to arcane distribution, according to tumultuous rhamphorrori in which salts and almonds quake and rebury their dysphonias only to emerge by parallel cauterization. Huertas erupt according to different rates and stages. Because they are beings they ignite from what I'll call intrepid occultonics. Occultations which accrue by means of a cosmic secondary charting, which discloses at a hidden stage a violent and irate monology in the character. The latter being one sow or one lemon erupting from a vega. Energies reflective of peat soil, being shallow, disinterested, combative. And it is to these combative energies that my light will kinematically converge as omphalos.

And if these tensions are analogous to the human state, its genetic longevity seems unstable. The Gods they worship instigate slaughter stealing from the Sun by advancing their own deceit. From what I gather a particular God sends out edicts from Lisbon and Rome, which in a circuitous way poisons the huertas. These are nightmare edicts which increase themselves through destabilized humidity. Within this condition genetics are distorted, and the mind becomes tense with genetic pauperization. For instance, if I once ignited a bulletin of kings, and then within a more devolved dimension was forced to burrow in a vega, anger would tend to root me, to pull me into a power of disruptive candelas, so that as a mystic or a shaman I could no more advance the Sun through orthogonal mathematics.

In this regard I advance my light according to an energy which transmutes according to the scent of rebellious quickening. Which in the quaking of human thought becomes synonymous with the literature of vertical rubellas. And names come to mind such as Lorca, and Cervantes, and Pessoa.

So as El Nath, the bull, the teeming insistence, "The Butting One," I uproot old tensions, casting from my presence the staged events of old rotational armies. Thus I advance the geometry of transparence, the scattering and re-synchronization of wolves, so as to allow huertas in their greatest sense to re-erupt in a Nilotic tenor, to advance the Sun and its tenets according to nucleic transfusion.

El Nath: The Immeasurable Number As Wave

As suns, our reality subsists on the non-measurable as function. And in this we all agree that our electrification exists as wave, as impulsion. Altair, this remains your circulatory phonation. Bellatrix, your auras burn to its music. As well as myself and our brother Alnitak who has not yet arrived. Mirach, within the tenor of your philosophical phonation we speak over and beyond regressive wavelengths of dust. We have coalesced through hearing. Mirach has allowed us pre-abundance, has brought us stampede through audition, as in-choate light rushing towards emergence. Not that we don't ignite as singular emission, or careen as isolate properties as appalling temperatures in the indefinite. Because there exist different waters in space, we have gathered together in this Nilotic rhythmos so as to understand all the differences and origins as one. We do not argue from fate but as seamlessly parallel enigmas.

According to pre-abundance, no distinction was emitted, no peculiar test of carbon, none of the fuels in projected hydrogen lakes. Even though I hail from a strange incendiary maze, I understand that we exist within a magical transverseness. Within a liminal range, not superimposed or ignominiously scrambled, thereby lending an energy to our rays, provoking a tenor of conflict. As if we mimicked conflict between Aztec and Hindi. As if we composed rumours between Tagalog and Danish. None of this occurs in this state which we occupy. We profess no such dictation, nor do we stress linkage which propounds strenuous instigation. We advance no peculiarity through reason. We are simply solar masses absorbed with signals from terra firma as evinced by illness from the Sun. Because of sentient peril on Earth we hover as in-doctrinal surges, as points which erupt through merismatic quanta. There is no need to question, or self-ingest dementia so as to somehow sustain an aggrandizing climate. We do not annul or self-position so as to probe at partial levels, which would leave us weakened when excoriating ruses. Bouts of slavery, certain gematrias of constitutions, where pointless charismas are enacted, which inspirate torture and monarchical substrata.

Because I do not seek to explain myself within the tenor of numbers, I cannot decompress my rays, and justify my species as a subtle type of warren. Let me address any ironical kind of naïveté tinctured by a proto-calligraphy which tends to punctuate exhaustion. Because I've never erupted as such, I've created for myself a second state of density, and it is through this second state of density that we explore our salubrious destiny as collective. It is through this means by which we differentiate and gain our differing states of enigma. In this, we are symbols wrought by boiling gain, as we combine through unregulated drafts, through diacritical subversion, much in the way that numbers organically burn and erupt from their ashes, in order to resurrect signals which respire in the pre-organic. This is what I'll call the uncertainty of basic physics, which becomes a confluent embryonics, which enkindles extinguished strata.

Say, I make a chart of argon rays and take as example an exponential number, darkening it across several scales, and several things occur. First, the root of beauty is occulted; secondly, solar flame is conducted through meta-conjunction; at a third remove, uranian entanglement ceases motion as estrangement. Therefore, in terms of an electric, or singular conveyance, let me post a thriving inexhaustible distance which under threat at a peculiar scale hovers in the soil and gathers strength during an unacclaimed transition, becomes multiply lit while magically conveying itself as ghost. This, of course, is not an erudite manoeuvre, no crystallized lesson taut with symmetrical antipodes. Because being and non-being are charged with decibels anterior to their own existing. So if I count, say, according to anterior motion, fusion is condensed within itself, which brings the mind to the aporia of display. Then gnostic reasonings awaken to scale, to rife or scalar instigation. Thus, the instantaneous self-replicates and creates for itself a fuel for articulate vanishment. And this vanishment is simultaneous with a residue of cycles where the tenor of rotation evaporates in the very coalescence of the aforesaid rotation.

In contradistinction, if a fractionated number is broken and sealed away in parts, and those parts are sealed away in parts, no anterior cycling can transpire. No salt, no counted vines, no chemical reaction. No connectivity to source can be maintained. And because no connectivity can be maintained nothing is left but an exomorphic weakening, limited to conveying number as outward unfolding. What then transpires are signals from the deleterious. Which tend to respire in the soulless micro-device which only simulate reaction. This being the reality which pervades the common populace, which means that all the heightened numbering are broken. No spiritual yield can evince its translucence from an anterior state torrentially fecund.

As differing stellar lucidities we cannot claim each others' strengths. Altair, you exist as something other than Procyon, or Aldebaran. Birth has given you a phenotypic "Blue-white," containing vibrational titanium and iron, flecked with the yeast of magnesium. This is your scale according to visible number, the draft which is oriented by your highest concerns. The latter which erupts as your telekinetic connection to the Sun. As El Nath I exist as a different visible garrison "Blue-white," charged with more visible size, concerned with a different orienting tenor. Like Mirach, I am second magnitude, and like Mirach, we are many light years removed from the huertas of Valencia. Because I channel different geometries of ether my modes exist as a different blue-whiteness than that of Bellatrix. Yet we concur on unsought data, on bursts which illumine beyond our powers which dwell at gross concern. Since the aura is in invisible balance we understand the enriched phonations of Mirach, of his telepathic phonemes, of his charismatically cleansed elixirs, which emboldens through salubrious hypnotics.

By listening to the mirage of one number, balance seems to occur as simultaneous language. Forces exchange, distances comingle. Mirach, the "Yellow-orange giant," who transcends relativity, who creates from audition new elements, which now haunts the human nucleic with alchemic nutation. Which tends to clear the void of poisons, so that the present huerta of beings can re-live and resurrect, and re-live and resurrect, and come to a virtue no claimed man can venture.

El Nath: On Inaugural Formality

My attempt at this instant is to express the exquisite layers of the singular, the inverted momenta of the integer, rife with anterior kinetics. Much the way one crystallizes sea flecks the anterior exponentiates, and divides, and implies, and gathers ghost informatives. As if one could capture a solar congelation before its first rays were combusted. Perhaps one could call it a moon burning as a doubled lepton arc according to shadows that shift, always osmotically invigorated.

I ask, what is it to be suspended by two shadows, totally unlike a superimposed finality? Not a feral route in terms of visible ramification, or exhaustion, or rumours from splendiferous sun reports. As for the latter, it cannot be assumed that what I say is of a strict or cosmological inversion, weighed in some rarefied extension as a proto-substantiation which portends a heightened visibility as clause. Because I do not argue from wooden flames I am not attempting to balance the pre-edenic through a reasoned form of dalliance.

Say, each phoneme constitutes the poise of a balanced fraction. Certainly it is not to curate anomalies, or to create an emptied pattern only to deny its substance according to an a-priori contrast with the invisible. Yet this is not to say that number according to scale has no reason, or conducts no energy within the evidence of itself. If one transects on the smallest scale there exists within this spectrum neither the anterior, or its thanatotic post-inscription in terms of its resonant evidentiary moment.

But if all evidence is sealed in this manner, what do systems provide, what do anomalies signal?

Perhaps at one level, flaws, or at another, divided incantations. Thus, draughts are advanced and measured. Signals are crossed at the acme of assemblage. And by assemblage I am not speaking of something evident or rectilinear with finding. My light being simultaneous with the way that leaves erupt, the way that lorikeets ignite. This is the Alhambra,* the Pyramid of Cheops,* the visible glossary of perfection. Not that I'm creating a convocation of hives, bereft of themselves through organic hesitation. In this sense the visible world is not a terminal application, being a reactive scent, or energy which always hedges by withdrawal. Any carbon I might summon from various invisible draftings takes on such shadings at the extrapolated level. This being the case we know that the visible is not the completed tenor, or advice imparted to shamans as if they replied within the limits of ordination. The latter understood is wisdom grasped from the simplistic, as if an atmosphere of signals condensed itself from natural remains. Perhaps a leopard, or a mountain wave, or a corona which ascends for worshipers at prayer. This remains for me the conundrum of confined response. Integers which accrue and naturally self-reference themselves. But again, in the deeper margins, I continue to contend that the fount of mathematics erupts from anterior origin. Its visible amount being the dialectic of its-self, knowing this respirational conundrum to be the embodied wave, being the intuitive scent of limitless hydroxyl. A fuel which I'll reference as verb, which consumes all fragments through its means as human realia. This being knowledge which is known on Earth as consumption of disciplines. Within the human ambit I respond to Moorish consummation in the mind. Its kinetic decimals, its range of fecund astronomical salts. For instance, if I as the Sun were condensed to human anatomical forte, and say, my blood were out of balance, I could retire to the bimaristan for medical consultation. If one were so inclined one could creatively respire over draughts, or cleanse the body as one preferred, or compose the poetics of song like the heavenly Walladah,* daughter of the 10th century Caliph Al Mustakfi. Rice and herbs sprung forth from regions like "Selba"* and "Elvira"* and "Shulayr,"* and "Gaudix."* Spherical trigonometry, "fitted megalithic masonry, in Lixus,* in Morocco, in Gizeh, in Egypt." We are not discussing methods which were sourced from combusted lilies. Science was harvested. The growing of rice, the treatment of hernias, so that study ascended beyond thought which succumbed to the centrality of schisms. Because, to be controlled by schisms is to hover inside a poisonous equidistance, which cannot fully engage the unification of thinking. The latter being the human paradox and its toleration with living. It cannot plunge into the suggestive, and create from its findings herds of invisible salt. It cannot deduce from the rhymical glottics which penetrate the linkage between the cells and infinite stellar rotation.

Therefore, in no way do we equate as brutal denizens, as interlocutors consumed by futility. Therefore, revered deliberation ceases to apply.

Aludra: On Anonymous Energy

There is tension, Mirach, between the Ground and what is called eminence of the absolute. This is constant, this remains as existence on the visible planes. Because I do not feign the absolute, I do not mark myself as its rebus as it ignites its consistence through fragments. True, as Aludra I burn according to hailstone figments as if I were a Golconda of fire suddenly scaled down to glass. Because I do not summon nostrums, or bear within myself a piercing triangular solace, I hover over phenomena with neither ire nor reverence, condensed by an assaultive tenor mixed according to a partially wrought alchemical means. One could call this the mark of distorted reference, or an emblem which sponsors force through in-direction.

As solstice, I have power, I carry in my distance higher assaultive range, yet I am not arguing for an eminence which sweeps the suns aside, which balances void against void, absence against absence, so that even suns spin against themselves, and ultimately contend with the utter rigours of anonymity. But there is something over and beyond the energy of such contention, it being the Ground over and beyond the autosomal as registration. To this degree, there is an absence of tenor in the way that carbon explodes, in the way that phenomena are released. And the query suddenly appears of how origins extend, of how the transparallel communicates with origins. It is like reacting to the memoir of one's forces across the scalar length of inverted osmium ranges. At one remove there is doleful in-sonority, at another, a picture which accrues from collapsed audition. So again, the questions are asked, is this a transitional relativity, a disabled union with compendia? Or is this merely a chimerical tribulation, or a sullied reference due to burning mis-impressions?

Conditions are always tangled. Even galaxies at times go missing. Yet, in other galaxies tornadoes transpire, and other absences occur, which are prior even to the penultimate of their anteriors. All is anonymous energy.

So does there exist an unconditional anterior which subsumes all subsequent anteriors? Or are there specific anteriors which signal vertiginous requirement? Then the double question arises: can the human state shift to such alignment, can it inhabit the range which extends beyond its own conduction as cellular apposition? Can we as specific solar embodiments combine the history of human ruin, with the life beyond life and its residue of bitterness? I am not seeking to reattach symbols to the lingering poise of those whom the human mind considers as chronically dead. To create a combinatory vacuum where transmixture combines ghosts with living familiars. Nothing arrives in this regard. It is not the compacting of animals with spirits. I am thinking perhaps, of a trigonometric being magnetized to the abyssal. A being who continues to respire by inversion in order to further comment on general disruption. If such a state is given energy to persist for millennia why cannot another level of life be pursued beyond the limit of human vehicular abandonment? If this latter state should perdure for 3000 años we can begin to say that a certain maturity has been gained. With beliefs dissolved, with familial potions transcended. At such a remove its spirit osmotically blends with perpetual non-confinement. This being the state which exists through anonymous conveyance. A being capable of life beyond any prior or deleterious instigation, so that the nature of what the scribes call death does not repeat its italics within its psychic depth or its free-standing judgement. In this sense the inner scriptorium is engaged at the cusp of beatific anteriors. Alchemic clairaudiance, wayward occurrence burning through limit. This is the understanding of agitations which exhaust the zodiac, which, on the face of the Earth, disadvantage empires. This is where the pantomime of rituals takes place, where currents co-translate currents. Gusts, deconstructed timings, thereby rising above the hive of advanced study. Because we know that each ray of study continues to advance through different temperatures and levels. Its ferment being not unlike utopian mathematics, or living symbols from Shrangri-la. Which to the current mind creates cartographical dilemmas. For instance, witnessing rivers of diamonds or carbon flow in full ascent. Perhaps seeing the Sahara as a green sea of glass, or listening to scorpions chatter in the language of zircon, like irregular cyanoethyne glistening with scintillation. So since this being from the abyssal has lasted for 3000 years, its powers are not shaken by fatigue, or any former example of itself as weakening. I am not speaking of Pharaoh or a body which assumes its power through context. I say this, because I understand the nuance which shifts laws, which tenders unrivaled conditions. An opening occurs, life gains itself through broken embodiments.

I am not announcing myself as such so as to forcefully retain absence, to make the origin of my advancement an intolerable singularity which simply opens and closes itself through abstraction. I am a sun which has come to intervene for the Sun distressed as it is by the fact of nervous ailment. As to the populace on Earth I understand its nervous insecurity, its ungainful mirages, which de-solarize spirit, which magnifies the fact of spiritual thrombosis. Mirach, I agree with all your levels when you speak of Nilotic scarabs, when you speak of the unstinting calculus of crows. This has never diminished for me, or spoken to me according to uneven principle. Yet I understand at this level cosmic entanglement as regards the state of being which invigorates anteriors. Again, the state of being previous to helium, which exists as the unintended. Mirach, I agree with your advancement, that human skill had been de-enlivened and corroded by minutia. This is thought which has been advanced through devastation. This is being occluded from being. As if the conclusive study of microbes or ophthalmics could renew the very principle of origin through isolate figmentation. I agree with Nilotic tenets that explore the body back to its origin. Tenets which explore the molecules occulted by hiddenness, so that the higher cells could explore through this hiddenness. This is how the void is subsumed by the body, so that the body and the void elude density, completely non-aligned with a-pirori purpose. So that celebration takes as higher revelation the fulgurant as destiny, as a maze with charged existence, which has no other recourse than flight to the unbelievable. This is not the mechanics of posture, of in-bred simulacra which reveals itself by figmental misguidance, the latter procured from a mind scarred by provincial misnomer. Such isolated representation being the confused semi-animate drifting magnetized no deeper than the mentality of material toleration. The general mind goes no further than a block of ice, a replicated convenience, or a rivet in carking holocaust machinery. For want of a better phrase, I call this the level of the unwise, this being the mind corroded at a debilitating juncture. Which means the neural field is trapped, and at best remains a dazed oasis, self-vilified, scorched by trenchant confusions.

This remains the mass of thought which I consider unqualified to live. It remains a tense and unlasting scarcity which wavers at the cusp of the uncertain. Sterility transpires. Hypnosis delimits its power within objects, which provokes in such a mental ambit a general source of identity. For instance, an Emperor seems to own his subjects, he makes up judgements, he executes offenders, creating in his wake monomial ungladdening. Such unhappiness has contracted into the power of the State. Each and every act takes on the power of a parallel hypocrisy, of all that proclaims breath within collective identity. This is why corpses continue to lend themselves to themselves thereby setting up hazard by means of magnetized disruption. Which means that the majority of souls agrees upon death, degree by improvident degree. They gorge on closed priority which advances its schisms through prior assignation. One could say that this is a prior or in-evident foretelling, perhaps something advanced in the Fornax Cluster, or sown in the subconscious state from dwarf companions in Vela. Such a state of mind feeds itself as pure fertility by arson. It is like multiple contagions viewing themselves from contiguous awnings. And these awnings, of particular hydrogen and carbon, partake of the same basic scale which continues to ascend within meticulous blue complexity. Thus, the simultaneous returns to itself according to the wave which roams as non-transfixion. This is assonantal energy, crepuscular storage, suggestive transcription, which dis-identifies and reclaims its own substance. But this reclaiming is exponential, fulgurant, flecked with powers analogous to various states of the unknowable. And this is not philosophy as acute irregularity, but dimensional transference, which alters its findings within the midst of embittered harassment. Yet the circumstance gnaws and appends itself to the dis-locatable as boundary. This in no way can become its meta-position as form, as blank chalcedony, tending towards the light transmixed in heaven. Addition cannot occur in terms of a crude or presumptuous stationary form, or a loose proportional epic.

Initially its synergy must know itself as disproportionate ray, and this ray can never cohere as a sudden positional motif, yet this is how initiation transpires. Not goal as summation or limit, or source which compounds itself according to pillage. Because I have not come to life as a riddled dromedary captain, I've come to this utterance through simultaneous emission as utter tendency towards the magnetic. Light being the language of utterance, these logograms spell themselves through quanta, constantly spewing from a well of atomics. If this be the case, Mirach, we are at one in this state of collusional rowing. We have come to the principle source as compatibility through kinetic. Therefore I've created my own response in accordance with anterior meta-topology with an energy which ignites its referential morphic.

I, Aludra, cast across indeterminate chroma, into descending levels of abstracted likeness, so that colours enigmatically emigrate, and branch out, and restate themselves through metamorphic warrens. These warrens being kinetic, there exists no pressure to stabilize their position to stalled psychological components. If I were reduced to being contained as a human vehicular embodiment, I would continuously create myself by the insolutional. I would take on a cataract of ideas, and challenge my own substance by debating them, debate by intuitional debate. This would be the salt of my reverberant intensity. Saying this, the sound which informs my continued living, does not elicit the canonical, nor does it undermine the means by which I escape from any postures I may have known. Therefore I do not debilitate myself as model, or as thoughtless impact basin or depth. I do not presuppose my own substance. I am not as you, Mirach, or as you, El Nath, conversant with the same personal synecdoches. I differ. I could never be a riven sailor coming back to life from a random charnal house, self-bequeathing my own suggestion in order to enter the fray provoked by quotidian havoc. I have no use for this type of susceptibility, as if being prone by a certain ruin, stoked by self-sedition. I am a sun who fuses alien vicinity, but never in terms of Earth and its provincial misanthropics. How many moons does it carry? How do its cycles trans-breed? I ask this, Mirach, because I've come to this vicinage only known as the unknown. Again I ask, how does its solar system fragment? How does the grace of its atoms perfect as perpetuant consistency?

These are not concerns replete with assignation, nor do they express or respond to insignificant outlay, but persisting as they persist as regards the present magnetics which implores me. This is a new and irrevocable thesis cleansed by strange amassing. Truly this occurs by the fact that the cosmos has no pointed or singular element that no voice appears as a region being singular over others. I've appeared, Mirach has called me by curious mantra from the oblique, never once stating my power through ritual, or at the opposite extreme due to inclusionary weakness. No, I am not of dire or corrupted example, nor do I provoke a state of medicines gone awry so as to invent and de-invent mysterious neural desiccation. I've come to re-deliver the Sun, to re-magnetize its workings according to in-specific sum, because I do not know the quality of the Sun from the Sun, I have not recorded the state of its spinning, as if I'd forgotten its calendric and spoke of this event vis a vis the inconsequence of circles. Yet I cannot reduce myself just to withstand my own rays, or befoul my own power according to the shape which evolves and prefigures translation.

If at one level there is a ray of dark ammonia, if at another there is the hydroxyl of exception, nothing can claim me as a whole event, or significantly deride my ceruleous or eclectic investiture. So as I've come to this Sun, to the aid of this Sun, there seems to be no place or condition for an anterior form of skeptical displacement. So I cannot trace my liberty by placing its function within obstreperous delimit. Within such range I can speak of no further example. I can speak in terms of no prior longevity or disregard. True, I understand that oceans are expressed, that the doors of moons are opened, that foment listens to itself through pure abandonment. I consider this to be the level where interpellation is disfigured, so the comings and goings of my cycles can never embody predictable embellishment. As to coherence within the flow of predictable Earthly enigma I have not found in my powers the reprehensible stature of those who embrace a prone dimensionality livid with illusion and fracture. Yet as I comprehend more and more of these dimensionless cycles I will more and more in-saturate with osmosis, thereby allowing its slightest degree to rise above the hominal fate which conducts itself through boundaries and war. The more and more they structure their belongings by means of symbols and flags, the more and more they imbue themselves with the perpetual style of slaughter, blindly drinking the blood from their own chasms, while feigning a strict embrace of discipline. This is one of the forms through which the Sun has sought to explain itself to me. This is how the hominal has sullied its smoke and lightnings. Because they have incited its angst, they have sought to fundamentally grasp repressive sunspot activity.

Starting to come closer to Earth and its length from the Sun, I am 30,000 years free of the Sun with the sum of its creatures transiting to another mean so as to focus at beatific comradery. As I speak a certain form of shadow exists beneath me. It is conflict burning through opposing momentums of flags. Always describing one another through the Dysgraphia of scribes. I have not descended from some chronic or utopian yield coming to Earth to describe disinterest, or to scale in several directions a stratospheric tundra, or create from an intervallic lattice a sum which re-enacts the dialectical form empowered by the carnivorous. This is not to test the olfaction of soldiers, or to gain on my behalf goals which are simplified through terror and reason. Because of this, artifacts do not expose themselves because my energies do not describe the Earth, nor do I project magnetics, which rules historic conveyance. Yet, I commingle with the humans, therefore my ethers suggest, and circumnavigate as sigils, as arrival from suggestive coma. Thus, my focus derives from unbalance. If now, I took on the chroma of dawn it would seem listless, it would be at the opposite end of covariance. Because of what I'll call a crucial meta-entanglement, each valence of light blurs with its co-principle darkening, becoming a refracted version of itself. Say, if I were a being at this hour, sentient, upright, able to amble on vertical extensions, I would gaze from insistent windows to see forms of blue hail staggered inside the body. Magenta and grey would combine and vary honed at some instant by countervailing streaks of vermilion. Thus, episodes would accrue according to various hues of saturation. As to dawn, there would be no direct or exoteric insight, no visible germ or principle carrying a signal. Yet, nevertheless, substance would advance. Luminosity would prefigure its own vitality not unlike the human mind recalling geese as a comatose flock of saffron. It is like dawn emitting sound from semi-circular canals. Much like a brief response from unbalanced predation. Perhaps ocular seepage as susurrant anarchics. Whether burden is enhanced through such rotative tendentiousness could only be proved by personal or subjective remnant. Only proved by the rooted instigation, the poise, the interpretive constitution, akin to wisdom subjectively kindled like phosphenes in mirrors. If I contend myself with such questioning, my energy would arise from buried dicta, strange, suggesting of itself energies other than direct or central burning, other than a chain of hissing stationary forms arguably pre-existing. Mirach, because I am unlike your original Federation, I seem to have arrived from the inclement, from a scorched or subjective forum no thought has called for. Your original electrifications I have not fully inveigled or absorbed. I have not been privy to its traceries or edicts, or to any of its forewarned or treatable osmosis. In this sense my energy has not occurred, I have not created traits for my own particular accordance. Again, as Aludra, I have not occurred, nor does my wisdom co-inhabit the aura which allows Bellatrix to speak of Saturn. Thus, I am outside of this particular observation, outside its scarps which creates alphabetic punishing cinders. Each cinder being a phoneme set ablaze by cosmic abrasion. And these abrasions lend themselves to the seemingly inapplicable, to warrantless assemblage which tends to confuse on first account, more or less like the in-referential as it manifests through sigil.

So if I suddenly turned into the anthropomorphic I would seemingly feed on a skeptical dosage of morals, thereby defending myself against hypocrisy and ill-reason. Unable to winnow dice, or build dwellings, my lasting strategy would be to sculpt abyss after abyss until all colloquial mastery would retreat into anterior causes, only to unify implicit dis-construction of pliant synonyms or patterns. This being sigil as acclimatized duration, the mind then being able to consume the anti-parochial as genius. It is like understanding the relativity of dazed adrenalin parameters. Or how colours are extended through concentration as exposure. How certain chromas cross-pontificate in fauna. Thus I cannot variate and thus do variate. Which is a paradox which issues ferment, which translates salt as if in flight, gaining from its registers magical intervallics, floating between microbes and the stunning interpretations of theoretical flaws and various quotes from a veritable range of incendiary topics. Say, of how the human plane appears in other forms and relegations. Maybe of how a quarrel may advance from rays and subsist within a badger or a lion for an incomplete duration. Perhaps I can speak of a bi-form, or a trans-measured cortex. As for potential on Almathea,* I cannot derive a codex from Earth, or create a geometrical locus which forms a dense or complex symbol according to the rising and setting of hidden coruscations. In this, maybe I suggest certain ethers on Ceres, or unforeseen conditions where tendencies erupt by blind accrual. These are energies which form within random or sub-dominate states. Because I say these things not with didacticism intended but with surreptitious expression never aligned to conscious vindication.

Therefore, I seek no approval from you, Mirach, I do not seek to join any pre-stated range, or become compelled to offer the Sun didactic resuscitation. Such is not Aludra, nor Aludra's orientation. I have not appeared according to dictates compelled by curiosity, nor have I come to re-triangulate vengeance on various factions of the human fragment. So that nothing can ever be due to one singularity or another. Nothing can be eternally immured in dialectic proposal lost in the insistence which functions as barriers. By rising above these barriers energy functions as great worth, as great symbolical invention, as simultaneous with its own kinesipathy.

I ask these questions. Does the Sun improperly kindle when the human mean disintegrates by schism? Do its neutrinos cease movement? And does this mean that I re-govern my rays through its history, through its motion as contradictory tonality? Or must I advance another system and work through new and unresolvable rotations?

By stating the above I do not resist myself, or take on unskillful tensions due to pre-ingested summas. Because such understanding has come to bear, I set up no rivalry within carbon, or summon disregard according to blank or dispassionate portion. True, errors burn, tensions are misstated. Whatever sum or particle goes awry, battles with itself and comes to no conclusion. This is how intensification is stated. This is how the nerves are thought to simplify. The latter refers to ancillary entanglement, to life brought down to a failed or corrupted persona. By erupting from the anonymous, I can heal the dead with my thinking. I can evince certain shadows from rock, and allow them to comingle as if to condemn themselves by momentary breeding. Yet nothing persists in terms of the fractions of human living.

As Aludra, my rays have never appeared, not on a single isle, nor have they been the root of any calendric, nor have they pierced a single tower, nor have they poured from improvident utopias to basely cook in wells. Which manifests themselves through basic unsettlement. In no way have I given myself dust to ingest, or plagued myself with fickle mechanics. So, in this sense nothing comes to me, nor do I induct myself with introductory laws as if I were forced to subsist by weighing moons in relation to a scorched gargantuan trellis. It is like trying to balance flaws in a second person defining disadvantage according to fraction, thereby, aligning the supercessional by balletic differential. As if life could only appear in terms of what could be called acts intrepid with errata. Yet, what I say is not a threaded wall, or commitment to persons. Certainly not a soulless advance, nor a bleak in-sufficient drainage. Because I do not shine on Earth there are no resins to declare. No mazes to withdraw or re-open. Nothing which gives power to staggered emotional kilns, or to listening to parts of gold scattered across damage. Because I do not sort my various planes of carbon, other conditions arise which allow a sense of seismic rotation several thousand years in the making. I cannot say that this is a lost or unscrupulous elevation, or magnetically reversed cinders which give off a prone or measurable imposition. In this I do not recall or attempt to structure or record names. The latter, like writing on a script of pre-Cambrian tar, thus projecting abstracted rotations as if thinking through a removed umbilical response or structure. Within such a state I repeat myself to myself by listening to myself through bottomless states of reflection. Therefore, if one immerses in such realia, nothing is advanced or divided as palpable conundrum. Nothing is convened and given fractional response. In this regard, the spark of the first measure reascends in itself according to primordial ignition. So through electrical strata there is summoned a-structural ascent carrying all the while sparks from bottomless gyres, which in a sense provokes human spinal flow by collecting Yggdrasil* vapours which creates by electric contact a field of uranian contagion. This contact is pan-specific and utters itself as auto-somal ideal. This being first contact with itself. Not laws or punishing claimants, or force by inaudible stricture. This is other. This is inaugural candescence. Because there exists no claim to pedagogical charisma I have not appeared on behalf of latent animals who stalk my inspiration, so that they can aspire to biological abridgements which require demands of lateral remembrance. For me, this is stumbling through base priority, speaking through fragments so as to ordinally self-endure in the face of catastrophic amounts of genetic indirection.

This is not the way that I've invaded this cycle so as to pervade the field with ordinal proof so as to prepare the mind for a prior or second amazement. This is why not even the voice I've come to inscribe will supply even as minimal evidence states which inspire drafts that extend from para-normal occlusion. As impermanent solar endurance I do not deny the power which subsists in raw involuntary form, yet I do not think of my rotation as mechanized salt, as mechanics of the potter. Thought ceases to remunerate itself as scarcity, thereby accepting my fate as something claimed from besotted inherence. Such are not tolls which claim themselves in a hazardous sprawling state. My light does not face itself through emaciated rationing only to give off fumes across an arachnoidal prairie. If this were the case, it would do no more than accrue itself as voided response, as unsettled interaction. My imperative is not stymied. Thus, the dawn arrives throughout various mists and strikings, throughout various chromas through twilight. As if stray magentas could travel through impeccable warrens, as if my body had reversed spectrums through its travels, as if it had formed clusters by taking on a micro-sonic sigil as passion. Organic imperative being the one compunction and its tendency towards that one compunction, duration being none other than a singular transmogrification. So if one phase within duration is a compound tenor, or an eclectic graph, or a tendency towards fractions, it remains the singular state of spirit which unveils and inscribes through seismic purity and force. So if I pass spell by spell according to what would pass for ophthalmic sources, there exist several states of tropic optimums. In this I do not repeal any tenor I have ever conveyed. Nor do I say to you, Mirach, that you carry no powers of utopia, or that you have lost the tendency to swell as etheric contour, which neither reduces nor stresses itself as in-bountiful allegation. At a lesser level it is like listening to moral telepathics navigate by blurred noises. But of course nothing is being conducted as if rife with mammalian investigation, or by the de-limited codes of a thrice-guarded ether, never given the virtue of unknown planes.

Does this beget in you, Mirach, sums of poisoned manna? Or does such sonance pass through you with a sense of in-beggeting? Maybe I'm sensing a calling which has yet to become complete? This is not to transcend you, or mis-beget your summoning the Earth to right balance. This is not to introduce a form as rampant scrawling, or to occlude by higher assault a chaotic manifestation. Perhaps at a certain inexplicable remove I'll combine a kind of kinesia with human neural calisthenics. This being exercise at remote rising, being something other than sedulity, or non-inventive day bread. Let me take as tact the leopard squirrel and attempt to resolve its methods on double planes. One, suggestive of the occult; on another, a resistive bohemia. The former is where the genes withdraw so as to arrive at themselves through tautology. This remains the root of the fragment as it burns in a state of mysterious oscillation. The latter, being the result of this mystery roaming at the bitterest of surfaces, where the phenotypic roams as phrenic tangibility. This is how we discuss bifurcation and agony. This is how the squirrel exists as a brief, but fabulous dalliance. But at a certain level the dialectic is thus ungained. Feeling is then equated with the rapidness of salt. So by eschewing regulations genetics configure as a curious roulette. By muting its very condition there exists suspended retoxification which shadows itself in the voice. Perhaps the journey of a vocal intensification spilling from the body of a figmental leper. This is not to strike an awkward balance, not as autonomous judgement, or as strenuous and calculating mirage. Apt response? Domestic configuration? I cannot say these questions apply. What I can say is that the second sign of the genes extends to blankness, to that neutral regime, which partakes, and enwraps fruition at depth. The outer body responds by spawning blemished oxides, by donning copals and washes. For instance, Spanish green, Ruben's madder, Turbull's blue. Then splotches of damson can be added, then Tyrian purple, then raisin black. Followed by ash, and ash gray, then precision by darkness.

It could be said that such a level is acute, and in this acuteness a provisional resolution may appear through realgar, through certain forces of Pompeian red. This is not a simple report from neuric atmospheres, I do not seek to stage mirrors, or propose a neural content that a certain populace would describe as apollonian expression. All prior habit ceases to persist. Mirach, this is something Bellatrix would know concerning his organic engenderment of auras. Perhaps this is a gainful understanding due to pre-existing stamina. Due to the fact that human life is not prioritized, or given dominance when posed against the powers which issue from the graveyard of the Sun. Perhaps uncarved emissions from sullen pyrexias, or interstellar pirouettes exposing its power as interminate example. Through respirational nomadics I cannot escape myself as alchemical locus, as thaumaturgic witness. Therefore I imbibe the anterior with all its prescient and unclaimed errata. Thus, I am vulnerable with radiance, seemingly pre-ordained with lightning powder. If, at a certain moment I speak to Altair concerning an in-rushing sailor and his atoms there may be a translatable lisp, or a pre-emergent access to the language of first tornadoes. Perhaps I'll find my light commingling with Phoenicians concerning cosmic innuendo. Perhaps they will re-translate the Northern bastions, or speak of land forms in Iberia. Perhaps this will flow into my carbon as a sub-annealed priority, evolving from seeming stasis a dazzling or photonic amplification, a unidirectional ray. I, the latter being a sun which escapes its preapportioned singular fate. Because as I commune with Phoenicians I'll know how humanity consumes its fate through risk. Thereby evolving beyond diminution, living in quest of erudite phenomena.

I'm speaking of the philosophical moisture in farming. Of how slopes were bred, of how marshes were spun, of how largesse could transpire through optimum latitudes. I am not saying that I know that total context of Iberia with its different fields and amphora. Because I do not speak in Demotic I continue to avert myself as a central or critical fragment, taking as my inference the thought of one concern. This can reveal itself through medico-centric blinding, as tragic compost within being.

So how do I know myself to be? According to the tenets of neurological exploration? As insight entangled within the fleeting laws of physics? I am sun, I am carbon, I am combustion through greater arrangement. I cannot erupt as constriction, or triangulate domains, in order to momentarily cease existing. There is something which exists beyond greater announcement. Because I cannot pre-figure my power by being solely constrained by embrangling ethers on Earth. At some level I am a-structural, an a-plastic witness to unreplicated intervals. I feel

I am witness, Mirach, to the code which the utter alchemists preach. To the code which subsists as intangible bullion. Let me say, Mirach, that I will commune with El Nath in order to subjoin auras which issue from Bellatrix. On Earth one could describe this condition as translating gusts, as telepathic insightment. This being error which reverses as transfigured assent. This being analogous to human form as neurological transgression splayed across a neutral field from which certain substances emerge as compounded scent. Thus, galaxies are regnant. The latter being energy which floats through general discipline, which illumines the eyes with colorful night ambrosia. Endocrine flare, sights from mixed osmosis. And so dwelling in being appears different. Artifacts no longer derive from themselves. No more do they warrant action to preserve themselves through an unprincipled nomos. They appear as fire as if sprung from a Mayan gnosis. In this regard Phoenician pottery is gnosis. This is how the first mathematicians explored and orated grammes. They understood ignition as powerful combinatory signs. This is how the acme of the Sun is dispelled through numeration. Not as an "aggregate of empirical recipes," but "elaborate and theoretical" comprehension* of all numerical eruption from nature. El Nath, you know the combinations of how riddles pose themselves through inevitability and degree, through circumstantial poverty, so that the highest allowable cogitation is reached. This, of course, is purpose which flows through free and inevitable danger. This being thought by alliance with invisible circumstance. So that tests are endured, logics magically frayed, then various weights are burnished by movement through subconscious dissuasion. Measurements are seemingly mingled and transposed as occult suspense. The result being perfection on the visible plane. All of our grouping must extend our rays to the "accuracy of Egyptian geometry"* on Earth. In this, the divination of the Sun was momentarily configured, so that astrological composure allowed the moon to darken and re-erupt as hormonal speaking in the body. Melatonin being the key unlocking subconscious reservoirs. This being unappended flow, clarified exposure revealed on the other side of ballast. Ballast being the body declared by oblivious observation. Yet, in terms of deeper view, the body as integral vivacity, as a combination of laws which soars throughout the multiverse. This is realia beyond utter motion and complexity which the present laws of the body cannot foretell.

What I'm relating here is not adventure obscured as private topic, but as energy umbilical with fascination. What takes shape by random degree are colloquies with hartebeests, with Cape Elk, with scolex crystals, with lupine forms, with altricial and rasorial vehicular complexification. Let me append the Karakul, the tamandua, the Syrian bear, as well as yellow dogs from Asia. And I can see an onager and an Angorra goat leaping over sullen wood mosaics. All of the above enacting nervous specification. This is synecdoche for the living nervous system, for its draughts, its habits, its conjunctions.

How does the body wander and procure deficits? Does it explore only according to monomial or direct aggression? Does it move itself through fictitious vocalization, or watch itself through selfless causational trees? Which means its very source enacts itself within itself through magnetic hydrational linkage. Yet there is and is not an unsullied source of optimum stellar attainment. As stellar compulsion I do not carry as thought the fractionated, the idleness soaked by indecisives. Therefore I can never be the ozone as prone and isolate integer, describing its somnambular instigations through strictly a-priori context. Because there exists breakage into merger which cannot be cauterized and squared according to objective substance. Because there is pen-ultimate tension between purest substance and purest substance, I being sun as floating omega wheel.

And being sun as floating omega wheel I'm certain that you will agree, El Nath, that there is no optimum finality as accrued from a lesser facility of optics operant on a plane of empirical contestation. You would agree that this optimum finality remains curiously self-assaultive reacting on all planes within the phase of annihilation. The latter being empirical value which casts its thanatotic spell within the dialectic of inversion and ending. It's as if our realities were delimited by forgone annihilation. It's as if proof our cathartic were stilled within a formula. It's as if our appearance had no other option than to exist as barren symbols. Which signal to the eye a barren thought report. Which gives as primary notion a barren shaping principle keeping our powers separate and averse to faculties, which transcends ordinal frequency as measurement. Its option: a pre-created mono-dimensional induction. A system which extends a basic psychic drought. A system prone to fractitious drift, to didactic impartings. Would you agree, El Nath, that such a state is nothing more than a morose or lost causation? Barbaric molecules. Exhausted axial mounts. As if being could be angled through composite amounts and resolved by autonomous thinking. As if principles could be derived from isolate compoundings and then separately embedded. Which creates a pattern of illness due to vertiginous with-drawl. Such delimited kinetic can never experience its own priority in a world synonymous with the event horizon. Such reduction creates no summons and attaches itself to polarized specifics. To sterile names, to denuded rejoinders. So only the parsimonious is stated, only peculiar episodes are advanced. This is what is meant by bereft integration, by motifs, stunted by ill affairs.

Mirach, are these the separative acts of the xanthrochroids, are these the results of their willful manoeuvres which only allow for meticulous reaction, to say, an abstracted botany, where even the Sun is conceived as a structural mechanics? Is this the principle by which their monarchs are rendered, by which their accomplishments are conceived? May I ask, do their thoughts proceed by punishment, and do the other forms of life seem rendered by seeming clannish appeal to destruction? I'm merely asking Mirach about total endeavour in self-torment. About thought which aligns itself to bio-mercurial congestion. It seems the human collective has been baited by such suggestives, and now discloses to itself annoying configurations, trespasser's ambits frayed by harassing coefficient components. Thus, a curious focus has been fueled by blazeless paranoias.

But let me ask you, Mirach, what is the living endeavour of this task? To help re-invigourate the Sun? To prolong the dominant species which breathes by means of the Sun?

I in no way pre-figure responses, or impose on the task calendric perpetration. The task being of such organic predisposition that movement can never be professed in terms of abstract or Imperial balletics. I have overhead and I have come from distance. I've sped as a fuel across a nightmare prairie, diverting random fuels from passing constellations so that I carry a multitudinous scent from various bodies across the void. Like you, I am second magnitude in this valley, this is why I've heard you, I've received your inference, the world in your view as medicinal drawing manger. Yet I've come to this condition unannounced, captured by philosophy which resides in pure intention.

If the Sun is in the midst of its billionth, or 2nd billionth year, how is it not strong, how is it that we advance to capture and transcend its ailment? I know that we have come to unite in ascendance to transmute certain poisons in its telepathic make-up. Thereby dispensing with certain elements in the populace which at present spin as dazed coherence. And this indirection has become an assault upon the Sun breeding a kind of fog in its rays. Thus, human life seems engulfed in broken instruction, which has led to the present state of general vampirics. Of broken body against broken body, of tortured feeling against tortured feeling. So we have come to heal wars, to evaporate generic conflict.

Is this illusion? Or do we shine as hallucinogens of the Ground? Or do we solemnly erupt as micro-comments through power?

Possibly Altair can speak of persistent optometry, of photopias which seemingly adjudicate and then soar beyond riotous minerals, beyond megalithic convulsions, as provisional powers of the Ground.

Do we mingle with the Ground, to delimit the universal construct? Or do we take a portion as summary to enact on principles accrued from invasive remarks? Again, is this rootedness, Mirach, or is it merely a philosophical phase which aligns with sudden transitory yield? So do we consume our own power as flooding, as ultimate act enabling disservice? Finally, is this moral fractionation in the void?

Again, I will listen to Altair as he speaks on optometry and hydroxyl as he re-inscrutifies the wastes of the intercosmic. Perhaps this is the way that deafness grows. Perhaps this is the way that grief or hail occurs. Of course we know that this does not pertain to sociology or pragmatics, or ensure in acts of daily labour. Yet fuels breed. Lizards mate with lizards. Forests extend as numeric exhibits. Then perhaps, a brief or utopian occurrence within the practical skills of a gross environment. This is not to say that we've magically expunged fate in order to clinically augment margins, so as to open ungainful necessity. As Aludra I have not arrived at speculation through dearth, nor through pedantic invariation, only to repeat what the Sun has endured. This is not my reknown, to speculate on strengths, to renew old fables through illusion. Parallel to this I cannot say that what emits from my rays is unlike doleful isolation. Maybe I could accuse myself of omni-dimensional simulacra, of igniting forensic or inhuman chance. The majority of the human species would say that I loiter, that I am immersed in post-intention. But I can say that I'm not scaling myself as a separative art, priding my species as an intrusive or cataclysmic ammonia. Though I exist as the unexpected, as the passer-by, as anonymous witness, as a gargantua who exists at the core of sensitivity. Because of this I am sensitized to moons, to energized locations, to inalienable respirations. If I attempted to count particles in this present task I would arrive at no gain. I would inspire eruption as a new and afflicted disorder. The latter being how science persists, always summoning from havens which subsist by means of strict logistical mirage. Always attempting to scrutinize phenomena by descriptive local pattern. The way an owl works. The way a neuron exults its chaos. I speak of these symbols as magisterial inversion, as an observer who speaks of a chamois or a sheep, or a view which remotely lengthens, akin to a serpent's eye, or to spells that flicker from photonic mountain ghosts. This is how the natural sum on Earth is beginning to encircle me, tuning my dazed affirmatives through darkened outlets and gardens. I know that I am contiguous, Mirach, that I am member of this sonic hamlet, that I exist as mysterious advance, that life reveals me through magnetics as bravery. In this regard, I may qualify as Hersetha, as someone who susurrates health across provinces, as presence who converges the dust in the ocean of emptiness, thereby inscribing a piercing occultation, inscribing the torments and revelations of heaven. In this I probe the secret metaphysics of depths, as mysterious instructor of "All Lands." As Hersetha,* I would stride through the "Double...House"* as witness, my forces compelled by intrinsic enigma. Within such a state I could say that the soil is just, and responds through alchemic osmosis. Thus I could partake of food or snow as example.

You see, there exists a human scale, certainly not conducted through indelible deficit. So I am not an alien transmission wrought by a fractitious or nameless in-discipline. As a Kemite I would sail into Luxor on invisible boats of tanzanite, upon movement of scorched magnificent water. I would know ports which contemplated signs bestowed by the tetragonal helix of the soul. And this is not a false or biased grafting, but an energy which can never stain or blemish its own making. Can never contain vain or hostile unfoldings. This being the scope which invades true phonetical audition by re-balancing water. Certainly not a cornucopia which inverts, which transmutes and enlivens beyond the fact of carking addendums. In this regard, I've come to light the Egyptian sea. So if my rays squint and re-consume, momentum exists. My reality understands this as a trapezoidal ozone, as an electrical anodyne which showers the Earth.

If I were a scribe in prior instants I would debate with myself in halls of electrum and discover elements of scrutiny within a rotating nimbus. Liberty, matchless action, transfusion of planes into planes. A continuous thriving no longer concerning itself with the life of devastation. Thus, levels are magnetized to levels. And by levels this is meant to be the stratospheric kingdoms disowning all economies. If terrestrial habitation evolved from such thinking, one perhaps begins thinking of the urban planning of Ibn Khaldun,* or the Moorish garden, or the "falcons of Valencia." As scribe, I would thrive on roasted sugar and salt. Other intake would include pomegranates, coconuts, various nutritional maizes, followed by oranges and rices ripened by intuitive bonfires and summas.

This, Mirach, is not to constrict within ancient dietary focus, or dwell within the enclave of Cordova within the isle of the year 960 A.D., with its 20,000 reading hamlets, its baths, its lighted streets, its exacting postal service. I ask, why would such illumination not have been allowed to grow, and take on exponential coloration so that collective temperature could have been organically maintained. Perhaps a trenchant understanding about the very nature of entropy and its gainless demonstrability would. I cannot give further detail concerning history vis a vis chronological proportion, yet we know that demise consists at present as the dominant inclemency on Earth. So one must go to the deepest glens, to the most feral enclaves in order to experience energy at its most persistent. Even though birds persist, even though the oceans take on the most serious of reverses, entropy kills, punishes, deflects, and creates through its tendencies, the merciless, the downgraded, the hapless arc which dazzles diseased collectives of critico-paranoia.

I agree, Mirach, that these are collectives which patriotically engender the blaze of their own regressions. These are the armies, Mirach, which carry the provincial code of moral stoning, which indiscriminately pursue usurious wealth through leprous activity. These are the models of the age, like a pointless torch or misnomer in the genes. Perhaps greater advantage would pursue if my rays were focused to persist in advancing emergent monotremes on Saturn, or resurrecting baffling cobras on Enceladus.

So am I persisting focus on pointless tests through phenomena, through making note of seized or extinguished records?

Somehow the void persists. I am one of its anonymous urges, one of its fragments which increases no significance, setting up no meaningful boundary. As stellar figments, Mirach, have we not tended to make a new life according to fabulous eccentricity. Yet none of us know where the dead appear, as though we were exempt from their tumultuous curiosity, as we evoke through the distances' tortuous trailings, or some splinter of ash cast from anonymous regoliths, themselves being scattered from pure electrical waves from curious regions from the multiverse. These are couriers from hives of interior optional forms, themselves having evolved from what I'll call the mathematics of unbroken n^{th}s. So am I shifting to one considered source? Or am I reconceiving the key to uranian paleography? Or must I centre on foreshortened optics theatric with desolation?

.

Altair, you are closest to Earth's heavens, you hear its mumblings by vicinity. Let me ask you; do humans strategize creating from their actions' parallel insomnias? Do they keep themselves structured by endless numbers thereby creating compound waking designs? Do they zoomorphically kindle integers according to meddlesome paradigms which threaten collective respiration?

Altair, do they subsist within energies which lurk with execrable omens? Or are they destined to devolve to semi-heated planes, which exist as neither planet, nor quasi planet, nor habitable moon, nor trenchant star?

I am asking these questions because my audition has conjoined with the bi-lateral, and by conjoining with bi-lateral imbalance a glinting erupts from my depths, which emits agitated findings, mystical summarization, which haunt the very cinders of randomness. Yet this does not alter the general fate that I speak of. The demise of my carbon, along with rhetoric that issues from mercury, and salt, and iron, which transfuses to bursts on the most nominal planes. I've heard all of you sounding as if you were igniferrous bells, as if your sound were in favour of redeeming life from fractionated symptoms. Therefore, we have no need to hunt amidst dogs to uproot injustice. We command the power of compressed rays symbolic of the multiverse infinitely permeable with option. Which leads us back to inevitable rooting by which the first gaze, the first cause was expressed. Yet this is nothing other than contact with a pre-existing rhythmos which is the meta-response of intelligence through telepathic current. I feel as if issuing from another gale of giants, from scarps of inward lightning, where the disparate concurs as a dominate blinding. This is where beings as solar forms exist burning as transmissive angles where separative pretense has no compunction to be. What on Earth some convey as mystical symbiosis, in other energies of the multiverse this is another summoning where entropy de-exists through dissolution of inverted vanishment where the ruins and species of the known have never existed.

If I were the Sun, and were to raise up dead Caliphs, it would not be to regain the vacuous, but to convey an electrical source which rises above the feral locality that has no other option than the form of rising and setting. What I mean by rising and setting are the univeralist's assumptions. What if the Sun suddenly leapt from this estrangement and conveyed this to Altair, and Altair conveyed this to Mirach, and Mirach conveyed this back to Altair, and Altair conveyed this back to Mirach, and Mirach conveyed this to Alnitak, and Alnitak conveyed this to Bellatrix, and Bellatrix sent auras, to me, Aludra, light would itself convey new alchemic significance.

Revelation?
Saturation through in-concluded unfoldment?
The Hierarchic subsumed within a-structural hieroglyphics?

Conversely, does this defamation of being continue through contiguous rites and lamentations?

Do I misconvey issues as they rise from a dominate suborder?
And is this suborder the electrical current of the most deceptive and heavenly disorder?

The Sun could say on this account that its existence and my existence are simultaneous, and that portions claim portions as though they were rapaciously plied by mathematic misnomer. Thus, we as suns could be soldered to the energy which produces human dismay. Perhaps this is how soldiers pre-exist before and after injury as though mortal relativity were the highest claim to being. Yet from another level or dimension this seems nothing other than as brazen opportunity, forensic dishonour, rivalrous disservice. And by disservice, I mean a spell, an anomalous blood-wish, which can do nothing better than traverse a suicidal death course, its mission symbolic with tarantulas and pillage.

Altair, you are closest to the Sun. Can you tell me if it's told you about beings on Earth who've arisen from death with diamonds in their veins? And if they've risen from the dead do they convey utopia in their findings? Can you tell me if they are rife for other cycles having bypassed the signets which erupt from euthanasia and corpses?

I do not ask you to invade the Sun in order to broaden your utterance, in order to transfigure answers. Because I've come from greater distance than this solar region I have yet to ignite the clouds around the Sun, with my realia being of unknown variety.

And you ask Altair, why do I not utter to the Sun directly, or continue utterance by irregular raft as if I were a partially imposed stasis seeking to ritualize wisdom approaching its substance through a burning or unspecified toxicity?

Mirach, I do not defer to Altair simply to persist as wayward solar alignment superficially engaged in order to provoke a-priori estrangement. I do not come here as the emphatic blue giant to engulf, to create a delimited ether in order that Aludra be known. In order to create a known invisibility which suggests me, which presents a perfect coalescence, a cell ferociously clarified by turbulence.

In my atmosphere sickness once persisted, my rays were scattered, my energies could field no emphatic posture, no code which could transfix prairies. Because of the salubrious nature of forces, I've heard the bell of Mirach which allows the mana of my light to cohere. Which allows the nth of my summa to penetrate voices, to summon up emphasis which allows the anachronistic to take away death. Is this not the case, El Nath; did not the fact of your naming emphasize the flight above defamation, the channeling which defines Divine result? So by concertizing inference after inference I have come to purest cartography by spell, to inner research working through the depths of referential mammals.

The latter being the coagulation of the unstated ray, which riddles, adumbrates, blazes, which opens depths, which reunites phenomena. Because the region which scatters between phenomena and essence yields to a disestablished nomos, which yields to the mystery of suspension. Which at times, creates belief in lost results. This is why Gods tend to appear according to localized pen-ultimates. This is what I call broken shadows, worship by in-direction. This being a cause of the Sun needing new strength, because suggestiveness has been subtended and de-empowered at the level of the facile. To a mind conjoined at such occurrence, a scarab is not more than a scarab, the occurrence of lions or rams is never understood or organically approached.

If I appeared as Ramses on an old Kemetic barge, I would understand the very salt of the invisible, the very root of its invisible discharge. This is the region from which the hieroglyphical springs. On Earth, this is a source, where the ferment of angularity springs forth like rays. This is where mystery singes and flares through inevitable crystallography that flows and spills beyond the rural as it's come to be defined within materialistic de-candescence. Say, in the language of Kemetic mystery each particular is known in terms of organic interweaving. In such a state, the Sun is not mechanical, the Sun can never function as ghost.

Does such thinking relate to Cambodian stupas, or to mist, or to transitional oscitation in the necropolis? These are not deprecations spawned as hidden solar charisma, but assessment of the jeopardus zone, of the present circumstance of its unique and perilous sterilization according to the Northern notions of rationalist anatomy. Heir to idiosyncratic Prussian anatomy where nature is classified by bereft and in-conjoined distinction, further contorted by principles which configure according to niggling frontality. The Sun now struggles with this myth, accruing damage to its dialectical transmission vis a vis this limit as human neural range.

Because I am here to aid the Sun let me speak of energies my optometry transfigures. Botany, flowerage, vegetation, grasses. In random order I think of mazes which magnetically brew as sea lentils, as sargassum, as confervas. As fuci, as rockweed, as lichen. I do not list them according to abstract classification, but as they occur within my field as angular mystification. Such mystification cannot regain its whole society by the divisive grammar of rational frontality. If I am arbutus, or bitterroot, or black-eyed Susan, rational frontality poses nothing but threat. Thus, the Sun becomes an ancillary circumstance, a post-positional occurrence. The same realia exists even as I reiterate analogous confervas through cineraria, or Dutchman's breeches, or Chinese lanterns. As Aludra,

I work through the energy of ghosts. I work through sporophytes,*
monocotyls,* plankton.* Through forage grass, through sedge, through
pampas, through llanos. These are aspects of paradisaical eruption, as
if life had seeded a lotus volcano through an in-rush of glaucescence,
which includes the farinaceous, the rhizoid, the carpic. Then again,
bloodroot,* azaleas, gardenias. Perhaps zoysia,* or durra,* or viper's
grass. Or calendula or monkshood. Add to this hartebeest, cape elk,
springbok; then the brush wolf, the cachalot, the burro deer. All of
these are noted, along with the mazama, the phalanger, the Congo
snake, the entellus. Must I go farther and speak of Andalusian hens, of
nighthawks, of stunning Arabian ponies.

Thus, the tellurian as aleatoric charisma, spawning at curious levels
of magical anthropography. It seems the atmosphere burns with
sacred alignment. Yet the Sun now laments the living form as energy
emitted from the ethics of ghosts, curiously surviving through inverted
ascension. It seems life has submitted to surrounding forfeiture. Thus
we've come to the broken conception of mortals. Perhaps Altair can
tell me how these mortals vanish. How they subsist upon a foul and
bewildering sediment. Of how they trade rumours through speech.
So the question is asked, have we come to both save and extend this
circumstance? And by extending this space do we create from this
yield another 1000 years of arrogance? Will we be crucial to enhancing
crucial and overbearing plagues? Will we extract from the Sun any
future subsistence? And if the Earth is not reached will certain aspects
of being suddenly implode?

This creates for solar form stirrings of sacred agony. It creates within our
kindlings a substance of solstitial morass. According to complexities

of stamina we burn at private limit. In the deepest sense we exhaust our own torsion, thus light is emitted through tortuous cacophony. So I am now thinking through inevitables, as if oxygen ceased to matter, as if the present phase of configuration was of immortal limitation. Experience within such embrasure is of the most feral lucidity, and creates such a collective remonstrance that we seek to expand our light to levels symbolic of ceaselessness.

Again, I ask: why, why at this turning, Mirach, has such an acme erupted in this region? Is it because the race is isolate and exists without living rejoinder? Is its living demonstrability a sentience which erupts from depleted concurrence?

I have not come to test this Federation by roaming as a strange or pompous aloofness, arriving to claim myself as the great Sun of the region. Certainly not askewment, or transfigured vertigo gone awry; or what could be called in the human kingdom a gangrenous complication within a forge of dazed metals. Perhaps it could be said that I'm not responding to acts of discipline, that Aludra spawns illness, that he is the very shape of disorder.

If, indeed the oceans can be saved from burning, photosynthesis will return to its fate over and beyond its fate complexified by staggered orientation. Then the moon will no longer leave traces of flame within random depths of water.

Will I, Aludra, be integral to the aforesaid correctives?

Will I create new arrivals of health by suspending dementia in the atoms?

Mirach, you must have felt by ascension through anonymity, my cogitation in blue mirrors. Therefore, I feel in my powers collective ascension. I feel all of you having risen beyond the telepathy of doubt, beyond curious laws, beyond empirical hydrangeas. Now, I can say that I'm the light which flows through ruined settings, through amorphic and compelling misfunction. Therefore, my energy is creatively un-alike with the black and ultimate failings which emit puzzles that roam through climatological twilight. Through that which gains through frictive in-concurrence, the latter being no more than the ice of what I'll call the state of immoral resolve.

It cannot be said that I provoke through clannish ruination, that I secrete the suns from my genes to provoke ulterior rotations. What possibly may come to mind is Delta Ophiuchi,* or Tarazed,* or Rastaban,* or Iota Orionis.* Perhaps they could be called erratic third magnetisms, perhaps the code of a private system, or incendiary de-cohesion. Yet when the human calendar goes dead will any of its light spark the delta of re-arisen response? Will any of its neutral bindings combine through telepathic suture and become brazen scotomas? This is not a revision or duality of the unforeseen. Yet, I'm only exploring optional rays, rays which are parallel and which mount in themselves as magical preface to the inscrutable. How further to explain myself. In a lesser sense to provoke lava fields, or listen to the worries in a voided polar stockade. To this degree, I integrate suns, with their nuclear transparencies, with their explosive helium counts. Therefore I gain a thesis which monomially explodes as glass, which blazes as alchemic spotting.

Being part of this local tremendum my ethers subconsciously state that voids have been transmuted, and patterns re-evinced according to colours which rise from impalpable saffron. As you know, El Nath, the Sun is of a saffron variety as if it were at one with the plain-spoken soil of Arabia. This being the dialectic of parching, called by scattered astral thinkers, fumes from blazing desert soils. But can these be fumes from the Podzols, the Chernozems, or the Latosols? Do I include the soil above the ice in the tundra lands? Do the Prairie soils configure through the different continents and their enigmas?

Need we know something more than this? Need we be mindful of illimitable forms of life through construction? Perhaps I must build further inference through hurricanes, or monsoonal winters on Mars. Perhaps, then parts of assaultive Asias, or Amazonian sums unrecorded in Brazil. Therefore, my light configures porcelain rivers breaking across buried realms inscrutably listed amidst copper tornadoes. Which transmutes as a beacon of rays, as a microscopic avalanche through selvas. Of course these seem as equivocal dictations, a frayed realia seeming to listen to itself. As if listening to anvils ring through hesitations. Yet these are not derivative portions of tumults resurrected and ascribed to veering ideas. As Aludra I can never claim to have arrived at consummate arrogation as if given insular chaos to dwell in. In this regard it could be asked why I have not included the powers of Adhara, advancing in its wake absorption of aetheric minerals. There exists no explanation, no reason for dwelling within a complimentary ghost. Not that Adhara* is particle, or invigorates its being at 3 times my exposure. Because I have slipped from Canis Major without trace, Adhara, or any other of the formations in Canis Major, knows that I have vanished, yet continues to burn as a ghostly scorpion centrality.

Thus, I cast light in doubled dimensions, thus cleansing the heavens with power that erupts from utopian corrosives.

Having said this have I betrayed Adhara, have I depleted the sum at the essence of Canis Major? Or is this sum the false tracery of negligible instants? Or do its stars continue to burn by continuous parallax and misjudgement? And furthermore, do the beings I'm now concerned with double over with old lightning and reverence?

The beings who now survive on Earth ambulate as electricity and want. Whose response to starlight varies. Who at times, demonstrates longevity, only to starve in spirit and dissipate out-right. So since I have not resolved the condition of entropy in Canis Major, how can the Sun reap powers that in complete degree I have failed to possess? True, I explosively fuel fragments. For instance, a being, heated by my heavenly transmission, may explore its essence for 500 years of dialectical transpondence. They struggle within themselves for a prior form of deathlessness, for tornadic purity, for an enigmatic ozone, which a cauterized human expression can't possess. And I do not mean to de-conclude the Sun of its power. To say that it struggles through evolutionary yield carries truth in that its possessive natural laws are writhing with transmutation. This is its sorghum, its grass, its empires. The struggle between stasis and longevity amidst the overall contexture of the remote. Which exists as kinetics on one plane, and significance on another, burning as dispossessive exposure. Yet I hear nothing from surrounding moons, or any of their rhetorics of alchemic fragmentations. Always it can be said that paradigms transfigure, ghosts yield their stations, struggles are permitted. This seems as agony, as destructive force, as argument. But this is how riddles dissolve through exacerbation, through tumult which derides old habit. Which complexifies, and proves itself through the ignitiousness of bursts through the ire of invisibly formed kelvins. Of course I do not speak through leper's indemnification, but there naturally exist more uranian forms of consciousness not deformed by futures in which only particles derisively hatch. The latter being the Sun and the Earth lamenting over broken gardens, appearing at present as useless of their own demeanours.

We know, Mirach, that the Sun should extend to the deepest regions of being, that it should foment and transmute all chaos. That it should slip through the forces of daunting cannibal's temptation, no longer giving vent to formless rioting in the genes. Yet, this is not to induce a totalitarian rule of conjunctive bohemias. I can tell you that beings exist in harmony with elements of old Kemet and Saturn. Elements which eschew the gathering of human blood by means of brutish implementation. And we know, Mirach, we know, that the Northern technocracies are always seeking to take the universe by blindness. As if the state of the Sun were translatable dust. As if provincial measurement of parsecs contained within their portions the very powers of the multiverse. True, galaxies burn, flames persist as example. But this is not realia which only lives through conscious response and representation. Mirach, to this degree we are not kinetic tools to be reported, or to work on behalf of a particulate hubris which seeks to extoll our very containment.

Which suggests an imprisoned osmosis, which suggests a blind or dictated principle that nauseates, which cannot know the fabulous sea or sierras. It cannot know an upper condition of cobalt, or seek the hidden forms of tanzanite and manganese. The boreal technocracies seek exhaustion by maleficence, according to the poisoned state of affairs, thus energy is deployed as disservice to itself. Written proof becomes animalized agreement. Violence always becoming the suggested aim, the traumatized decree. On Earth, we know, Mirach, that if we were both the Sun as the single Sun, we could have been called day star, or Shamash,* or Savitar.* Because our light does not derive from beasts we mesmerically cohere to RA of the Nilotic paradigm. And we agree, that the Sun needs to reappear in this former transrotation, thereby arriving at the 5th or empty season, where duality becomes less and less as persistence. Thus, becoming saturous with blazing. Being conduits of the multiverse we carry decisive uranian action beyond rules or opposing suggestions. Which means, the burden which eats at the body—missing.

So how does the body ignite such disappearance? Through growth from a fabled nether soil? As atoms alit at the doorway of the bizarre?

As the bonds of phenomena loosen, the cast of pure energy becomes evident. Interior transparency occurs. Increments flow. A perfect fluvial fire which osmotically glistens beyond occult embroidery. This being beauty which gives the Sun new feelings. Thus, there exists no primal distinction between the terrestrial, the a-terrestrial, and all forms of the cataclysmic. This being at such a scale cartography cannot follow.

I could allude to mystic translation concerning exposed blue lands, or to triangulated currents in dark pelagic wastes. I could say these things. I could evoke gesture through flags, or consort with my own carbon concerning primordial figuration. This being motion which ignites and spills out through fervour. Which does not suggest pointless mental posture, or superimposed belief. Say, if I included the human community by igniting oppositional enclosures there could never exist an approach to collective thought transference, or experience rays of relativity spawned by collective visceral ambrosia. I cannot project a summary of how the impersonal would occur, or how the anonymous would coil as transcendence. Because verticality is not based on the science of willful ordinal numbers. Because sequential foundation has never existed. Of course, we are not concerned with thoughts which frontally congeal and hover around a person. And of course, there exists a recorded criticality which exists outside history. As if the simple bones of a body were the only witness incantated through error or destruction. It would be as if I were human, grafting cards by creating provisional terminations within an umbilical conquian. Creating drafts and models collapsed upon themselves. As the human state presently commences, there is always available the crude definition by stasis, going no higher than unformed ideals.

Altair, you've overheard their concalescence, their mires, their stasis of force as anger. When kingdoms were new did the Sun know this anger, did it erupt through inclement retreat? What I can say is that the Northern dynasties have sparked nothing which implicates transparency through obelisks. The latter igniting ghosts in miraculous burial fields. These ghosts, being the primal realization of blank neuronal charge, their essence transmuting to flotational beams capable of life at all levels of possibility. Which implies human gracility as being replete with a series of states within its vehicular organics, which includes the realms before parturition, and the great conundrum within the aftereffects of living. The aforementioned are the two invisible states which function as the unstated gaze encrypted as uranology. Again, an energy analogous to the seeming statics of Saturn, to anonymous waves unlimited by apparition. Within human coherence a higher strain of this energy evinces itself as those eponymous abstractions beheld on Earth as art. Those leaps, those invigorating glossolalias which invade the spinal form with an invisible thermotics not unlike a pyrogenous eros. The latter being a kinetic which calls for the anaudia of infallible solitude, for astonishing immortality as study. Thought igniting feral turning angles, followed by absorption as ferrous ghost appendage.

Open states?

Neurological transweaving?

One must pass through mortal basics and arrive at the transillustrative. Not the heavenly state as implied by conventional noun, but the transverse integer risen above itself into newly inhabited chimerics.

Resurrection?

Mortal co-finding as hubris?

But at lower levels, anger. The result, clannish conversations in a conspiracy to reduce being, to diminish example. Thus, it revokes the spontaneous and shifts its influential body to circumstantial exhaustion. Our Federation erupts in order to breed the essence of energy so that definition by phenomena ceases to impede flow as it interfuses with the original field. This is certainly not a crude or willful angular commitment, but as subset of the multiverse, as a form of astrolithology, evincing a scale which induces dimensionless amixia. And so Dorado,* Caela,* Triangulum,* simply inscale themselves through anonymous direction. Perhaps a wave of perfect wisdoms sundering default, say, if I were sequential in demeanour I would be replete with the curiosity of Canis Major. I would speak again of Adhara, I would speak of Sirius, I would speak of Mirzam* and Wezen.* Then bring to bear the stars of Eridanus* and Perseus,* of Gemini and Canis Minor.* Then stars like Alhena* and Zeta Persei* would appear. Perhaps then, stars such as Procyon or Cursa would come to address us with new particulates, with new substantive magnifications, with new mantric calliopes of origin.

Can one call this illuminated frenzy, morphed a-lateral crystallizations?

It remains an energy which burns outside current planetary posture, beyond the mind which results through utter strategy and fragmentation. Which is not to derail measurement and accuracy as they culminate in sweltering world accounts. Or as they align themselves to mirrors of starlight. Bringing to account all the pictorial timings of suns which blaze in the Sombrero system, or the first Kemetic markings which soar as astronomical kindling.

Another force comes to life. A kind of fever is created as an evolving neurological fusion which coalesces with the unmatched. A dense and curious longevity transpires. A neural transmuting through struggle. Which equates with the unforeseen. Thus, the alchemist body as self, as transtructural aurora. Not inner storm by defeated bearing, not simply moons and emotions. This incites originatory powers, this incites the first true partaking of the Sun. This being energy which rises as hidden ocular weight. Which portends more than a lurking clairvoyance.

Quaking zeal?

Fevered astrological hamlets?

What I've uttered is a state of nerveless kinetics. Uncaptured dice, nerveless dis-burden. Teeming aural states which blaze. Cyanoethyne as a by-product of focus. Such inkling elicits its own arcana, the anthropomorphic becomes a state which morphs into non-definitives. And in a lesser state of morphing is less and less tenable vis a vis the optimum form of oxygen. A spectral form of breathing. This being the re-discovery of a penetrant electrical motif. Saying this, am I negating our present solar Federation, and the riotous molecule which we agree upon named as terra firma? Again, will we save the species from it-self, extending its gait across a 500 year life expectancy? Again, are we a hubris of suns, a particle of habits destined for consumption by exhaustion, only to be reclaimed by the power of the overwhelming?

Altair, can you evince this state for me? Can you compound the Sun so as to uncode its forces? El Nath, can you weigh its electrons? Can you splice its integers so that its light renews as unwhisperable linkage?

Alnitak, am I strangely concocting blizzards?

And of course I ask myself, am I simply a chain of suns within the Sun? Or am I a useless intruder operant with chaos?

All that I can utter is balance, as persistence as purity through balance.

So am I Aludra as mirage, as binomial shadow?

Because I cannot grasp the pre-judgemental, what I say does not cohere as graspable or frontalic certainty.

So again, why the population of the Earth beneath the Sun? Why does its torment yield torment and issue at no higher state? Why its neo-preponderance and sickness by abstraction?

Do its limits re-structure limits through its phenomena as grace?

Is this how its anonymity burns?

Is this how its theophany creates riddles?

I can say that the basic Ground is innominate, is cryptonymic, is isolate from actions which seep with extrinsics. In this sense reality is clandestine, and can be known through provisional origin.

Huertas, continental slopes, white caps, veranillos, visible horizons.

As suns, our heightened sense allows us to partake of the innominate. As suns though we grow xerophytes by scalding, we partake of the innominate. Suns cannot isolate fogs, or folded mountains, as if they were separate from the cryptonymic, as if a fumarole, or a geosyncline were to exist beyond a billion años as separative and demonstrative figments.

Can resistance accrue from such vehicular testament?

Therefore can any sun deny the Ground, the utter rhapsodics, which erupt from perplexity? Such is the incalculable state, the fermented prism in which no mortal governance is found. Therefore, the universal is local, is an extreme inferno of subsets, which then triangulates through oxygen to form the prevailing human galaxy and its forms. Thus, death and life in the human state become nothing other than a tense or forensic molecule which opens briefly to the unusual. As Aludra, it is my understanding, and only my understanding, that our initial acts foment the miraculous. And from this, we shape the fuel of new electrical warrens, that we adumbrate intransigent inscriptions so that they violate demeanour, with new possibility being extended. It is like watching a Cirrocumulus transpose intelligence into unknown regions of the multiverse. Which exists as other aspects that illusively transcend the retrogressive persona as it has known itself throughout acts of history. And it is only those moments which have transmuted to duration, being able at all instants to commingle with the multiverse.

As preamble I could quote our rays as moving parallel with quanta, as if we rode blue electrical mares through intuitive electron gates conducting ourselves as referential germination. This being ghostly solar germination, as if certain dyes were elicited, such as Victoria Pure Blue, or Congo Red, or Diazo Brilliant Orange. In a sense, dazed elements which fission, rising above exhaustion. These are rays having no action in forcing bread to grow, or residing in reductive predicament. Never prone to remedial stresses through conflict, there is never the energy which extends through a prudent secondary calling. So there is absence of insistent entanglement through recursion. Myopia being drained past its minimums. This is no longer a strategy which positions itself by rocks and blindness, by mirrors always plagued by extrinsic enigmas. On Earth, I am speaking of bodies suffused with streaks of zoneless surges, no longer prone to lexical residue, to emoting through terminal imbalance. Beings that the poet Dante could never conceive of, beyond any mode which encompasses behaviour as belief. Unlike the throes of Dante there exists no absolute example, no sudden and unalterable monkshood to bear.

Mirach, as this evolutionary nexus, we have advanced beyond neural indictment, so that aural liberty ensues, as if listening to a tracery of bells flitting through the powders of twilight. A convergence, a quantum in-scrutiny. Which exists at one level as elaborate insolvency, at another, those aforementioned mares, those unsolved exposures which drift through terrifying stages. Perhaps, this is analogous to the magnification of cells witnessed through isometric lenses. Not simply a brief or challenging mist which announces asymmetrical transmissives through stark electrical quanta. As psychological expression transmutes it will combine with this quanta transgressing all prior precedent evinced as psycho-biological nutation. At individual depth, an alchemy of floods, a crystallography of fires of curious Promethean beauty. Tornadoes in the blood, Aztecan volcanoes.

Am I close?
Have my rays so magically invaded?
Can the race now attest to such allotted suspension?
Have names been lost?
Have identities been exposed to intergalactic charisma?
Will cartographies then change?

Will Venus cool?

Will its Sun start suddenly rising in the east?

Is this the spirit which now commences as lunar nuclei?

Is this the Orion Spur speaking as Asiatic ray?

Perhaps this mimics the Sun too closely. Perhaps this too closely aligns with cosmic super-imposition. Perhaps this is local law posing as in-lit alien neutrinos.

Let me utter in another array.

Mirach, have you subtended blizzards of neutrinos?

El Nath, are stray parsecs apportioned?

Altair, what of the release of your intrinsic ghosts?

Alnitak, what of your fuels of higher comprehension?

And you, the Sun, can you answer within your depth's pineal light and its extension beyond the Perseus Arm* into the albino garrison which spirals as Andromeda?

Perhaps in unison you can sing of psychic oquassas as limitless teleology. Or of the unspoken range of scarabs and spiders. Because our rays have come to the "small partial arm" between the aforementioned Perseus Arm, and its counterpart which looms as the Scutum-Centaurus,* both having floated 16 times through the mist of galactic origin. Earth, suspended in the Orion Spur, exists within its portion of limitless obscurity, possessed of unknown stamina in the midst of perpetual drainage. Not that we've come to staunch the drainage, to assault the forces which issue from its cosmic valley, but to send signals which intuit the drainage so that another transmission arcs through circumstantial cluster. Therefore another state of ozone migration, which listens to itself as the dialectical foci of the blue lakes of ethane on Titan.

Perhaps these are false or morose habitations. Perhaps projection of collapsing insular rotations.

Mirach, I am known yet unknown and known. I know I am bringing the Sun beyond disadvantage, and I know I help crystallize the scent of our alien nomadics. Our spillage, which orients light as simultaneous election. Of course, we have nothing in keeping with summoned clerical lions, with technical verbatim, or technocratic selectivity. As to autonomous perfectibility I create no leaning or reference. Drift creates current, creates intrinsic realias as if a poise had suddenly evolved and stated itself as Jamaican nopal. As an apparition which poises itself through vertical osmosis, knowing its brief indigenous moments as an alternative chronicle of fire. Yet always morphing surmounting the chaotic as predictability. So, Mirach, is this not to advance upon the fact of a living origin, which sparks its signals even in motions which crawl as inevitable sub-species.

Because there exists no division we rotate at other levels than the ocean Sun. There is the power of random plentitude at the strength of tenacious crossings. And through the strength of photonic listening that I've gathered the currents of lilies and wasps of scorched ammonias and basins. Thus, I sense, I have arrived at aetheric rooting.

Mirach, must we carry the scent of the Sun? Must we mimic its fire on old coastlines? Or must we emit from our carbon first causes? Interior psycho-diagnostics?

Questions, Mirach, posed as a mural of dazzling galactic bodies. Bodies, scattered like intransigent fennel thriving as deciduous enigmas. To conventional apperception it is like gathering a deafening set of parables on the one hand, and on the other, attempting to absorb the states which shift as macroscopic parabolas. A circumplanetary language, being anagalactic solfeggio, being intersidereal audition.

This latter skill I know to be your domain Mirach, your compass of acousma. Because of this power, energy will start to cease moving as regressive unfolding. At minimum, as a-priori interregnum vatic with thaumaturgical fevers. Saying this, I do not glance at sidereal damage, nor do my rays defer to lessened drift, or to polymorphic negation, arguing from bio-intrinsic style or preponderance. Thus, absurdity loses its skill as utter resolution through matter. Therefore, the very essence of light erases its own destruction. Carking assignations, surrendered, jettisoned myths, no more than exploded philosophical debris.

Being human and consumed with the aforementioned, I could never refract as a delusionary monster, or extract from my bitterest components a marking, a terrified mnemotechnics, in order to cherish undue opposition in the genes. I would never listen to myself as a defeatist persona, or clothe myself within a form of exhaustion. I would begin to subsume forces which would assemble the selves against the mean of reactive trembling. Because I would have studied the general fire within coffins, I would assume immunity from perfect lawlessness, so as to sketch another fuel, another law of insufflation, thereby instinctively reacting to the a-mnemonics of inenarrable blue eagles. These eagles being as signs which roam through curious co-equational absence. Neither as mirrors, or fumes, or forces which re-instate summation. Which leaves the electrical field unmarked by geognosy. Thus, nothing remains of barbarous calligraphy. This would be the human element forming at another level of dalliance, freed of index, or the superficial fragment. The biography would take as its site the flotational scintilla, triquetrous with transparency. Such a body being the "Axis" which spins as the "Heavenly Door,"* as the quivering vitreosity as nascence.

There would be no longer the fixation upon fatigue, or the atomized persona searching for bleak directional stasis. It is at this seeming level of isolation that the body no longer stages itself as a precedence for death. It is no longer denial of the transimmaculate person, abstracted without the tenets of meaning. The latter then lifted to a mix of invisible green fires, mixing with themselves through meteoritic radiance. A living gain, not of farinaceous origin, or a composted spire composed of thinking, frayed by reactive frontal activity. Because at this level mathematics becomes diaphanous, and increases in the body chemistries which allow alchemical dialogue with the heavens. Not only an albino sea on Enceladus, but interactive ascents which pose and counter-pose with other conditions of remoteness. Which is advanced exploration through being. Which would give to the Earth a buoyancy in keeping with the biological climate as transmuted glyph.

Life is formed into another cycle beyond want and disadvantage, so the senses transmute and the technical claims of the moment become bereft from visibility, from any answer it might solve according to width, or toxin, or calamity. Being informed of the northern forces, we are attempting to transmute their basic tenets, their destructive dissertations, where environments create clauses which consume by annihilation. Our light, Mirach, will begin to cast relief upon beings such as the Scarlet Tanager, the Arabian Oryx, the Asiatic Lion, endangered inchmeal by inchmeal, not unlike the Zanzibar Red Colobus,* the Malayan Tapir,* or the Spanish Eagle. We have come to nutate the Sun, to put the higher plane in order. As to compound errata the microscopic emerges with its unnatural veering, with its magnification altered, so much so, that the Sun at magnetic apogee interacts with Terra Firma, with dosages or static, with cindered misdirection, which haunts the human pineal thaumaturgia with sullied magnification, with drift, producing in latter generations a collective frontal aura, which obscures the pineal, enveloping its powers in a feral neural cacophony. Let me say, Mirach, that this tendency to static has been increased by the North, so it has now reached a level of intolerable tension, creating in the spirit, riot and blinding, and all manner of dissonance. Because this dissonance is contractive, it becomes the union of all flora and fauna in death. And all the allies of death have now become as anarchic providers for a kingdom which now devastates its invisible sustenance. Thus, the general field is damaged, much like watching ice poisoned by flooded ink. The genetic tenor now corrupted by a tendency to announce its combustion through offspring sullied by epigenetics. The latter being error by compounded error which transmixes the unstable as imploded points of view.

So you ask, Mirach, what are these points of view?

Debris from old infectious planets?

The mode of schizophrenic rakshasa?*

Let us travel down to denser and denser human minutia. To shaping principles of human thought as destructive kinetic. Quantification; biology condensed by material determinant, by "observable" activity. All life being fueled by the extrinsic, by depressive construct known as monotony in the body.

The soul is constructed as bleak interior gulley, as carking transpersonal debit. The oneiric is at best considered a dissonant lunar embranglement, a characterological distraction, to be studied as paradox within the debilitating formula of conscious and subconscious bifurcation.

The proposition always provoked is the inducement of phenomena as reason. Which in turn attempts to explain the arachnoidal, the frenzied, in terms of what is called institutional normalization. Which leaves the mind gasping in the wake of its own disservice. Therefore, activity remains stultified, unexplored, frantic. Harmonization de-exists, the social diet, poisonous. This is an atmosphere which condones itself through the strain of concussive magnetism. Which registers curious heat, pestilential olfaction.

Mirach, we collectively agree that the species resides in charismatic depletion. That its general tendency has reduced itself and now touches bone. There is a skeletal disquiet, a blazeless foil which saturates the clothing. This has become the basis of speech, this is how roses are spilled to pass along their dead. As suns, we see an emptied summarization, a disabled kinesis scarred by various addictions. A condition which has dissolved and is dazed between simian and fish. Language has devolved to blunted signals, to anointed disregard. The in-cabalistic as genre, as promotional extrinsics. These are beings who never raise their eyes for fear of exhaustion, for fear they may miss the power of some delusional mote, or some curious befoulment due to moral inadvertence. It's like the bitter evolvement of wood in scaffolds so that literal bodies are hung according to constitutional imperatives. This is the struggle of the State to bifurcate justice, to take on the fatigue of dissemblance as purpose. A fatigue, with exposure to nerves, to oligarchical systemics. Thus, kings decimate their own addendums much like a riddled tourniquet as voice. Injured, hidden, deflective, seemingly occluded by rationalistic inscrutables, these surrogate kings think by means of penurious metal, by means of desecrate formality, so that fear burns in accordance with the need for inveterate immolation, always applying the latter by means of curious forms of insolence to the reactive gallop of the populace at large. Implementation occurs through a disfigured minister implanting affliction in the provinces, always perfecting himself according to the etiquette of murder.

Such is the galling nature of the devolved, flawed as demonstrative codex.

We watch, Mirach, as such pernicious ignitions transpire, soiling the general electrical state with destructive dispositions. Therefore, ruinous jurisprudence, trenchant recidivist maximization, with the preresolved intent of keeping a vampiric structure as harvest.

Mirach, can I contrast this with Buddhist water wheels, with undistinguished carbon flowing from the indescribable. Not motion unfolded through anachronistic stirrings, but a series of haunted vertical myths as penultimate or altricial seasoning, in turn giving rise to perpendicular currents corresponding in being to utopian kinematics. Which leaps the clouds from poisoned table clocks. Not a pointless optical plight, but vibrational inherence transfixed with the infinite. Because to be with and of the infinite is the elixir, the monos of blessing, flashing, combusting into signals, simultaneous with unthought momentums.

From this, perhaps, a vanished seasonal bleeding, with the squalls of the body beginning to radiate beyond a state induced by derivative grammar. The latter being nothing other than famished tendencies, psychic droughts, inverted fortnights, wrong construction on things. Hesitation is then stilled, derivative grammar is thus broken.

When the Northern mind constructs a particle of lightning, it never infers a triangular ozone, or a mist which rises and transmutes, and re-invigorates a constant parallel of new ozones. As Aludra, when I refer to new ozones I understand them to be as "described in the Brahma Samhaita as Vibhuti bhinnam." Being the infinite atmospheres of the "100,000,000" planets,* being blue suns, reverse volcanoes, amarillo waves. This being Jiva, the life force.

As suns, we are the life force. And because we are the life force, we shatter the flaws of vilified dynamics. This being the Northern spirit on Earth, with its fragmented inks, with its trade in terrible portions. This being the manner of recidivist thinking which tends to bifurcate the ultimate tenor of Chinese or Islamic alchemics. Both converged in seeking the Divine elixir, through the ferment of wonders, through the heavenly salt which seasons the empyrean. What I'm evolving to is the Ground* suffusing the Ground, where the Ground transmutes and becomes the inexhaustible. And as nature is so suffused, it rises, it takes on the power of its alchemic parent, which again and again never implies stasis. This is what I'll call alchemic uranian pavonics, an inscrutable light which spirals beyond all prior solar assignations. A-pontifical calm, salubrious erosion of malefics. Which stuns the forces which undue themselves by evil. Forces which name themselves dybbuk, shedu, gyre, and name themselves synonyms such as Aeshma,* Shaitan,* Ravan,* and Angra Mainyu.* These being the droppings of wereboars, of uturuncus. As if I were a servant cleansing toxic shadows from a burning river.

Mirach, our light derives from pure emotional ascent, advance by paradoxical advance. A height which rises out of opiates and spiders through codes, which issues from a rattled mountain jar. A jar enriched by nuclear solar feeding, which in the somatic state becomes a neuro-trans-sonics. Nutatics. The neural shift of the darkened cellular field. Which re-inspires, the Magrib, the Indus Valley, the states of mind known through the Ganges and the Congo. Which is the trans-personality, the spectacular re-recognition of the luminous trance of mystic powers. As to ambush as motive, as to planktonic error, none can transpire within this "supermost dexteriority." Which qualitatively dissolves any strife through umbilical gargantua. Be it Mimir,* or Ascapart,* or Galapas,* or Firbauti,* ties are dissolved, nightmares disserviced, squall as terrestrial power is broken.

History cannot repeat itself at this level. It cannot adjust, or foresee itself as ruthlessness by sprawl. It cannot respond by delimit to the ghostly intellection in the genes. History remaining an inferno of lessened constitution. A draft. A series of illusory items.

As suns, we can only profess unending resistance, being neither derivative from, nor available to dying. The being, Sri Ramanujacharya,* has spoken of the eternal energy of the Sanatan Dharma which exists as in-diminishment. It seeds all the blind formations, the exhibited trees, the ineluctable rays, commingled with ice and winds and seasons. Which lets my rays seep into the paurometabolous,* in which the nymph of the pauropoda is simultaneous with the maturity of its granulated counterpart. This is a state where general being is equal, where the parts cease to waver at one reclusive stage or another. Even in this lower analogy we again exist as the Sanatan Dharma, the everlasting which ignites as bluish ecological charisma. In humans, this latter state, is "the sound eye,"* the "eye of magic,"* the eye which transmutes "light" into "spirit." One is thus anointed by flames, by melatonic mystery. This is life, beyond properties of zeal, beyond prone or lenticular leanings.

Having escaped the levels of roving psuedo-wastes, we can allow the very nerves of the Earth to renew by rotation, to escape the human yield of suicidal sociology. Thus, beings begin to grasp the fundaments of the soul "in the brain's ventricular system."* Where the "spirit," the "soul," the "mind," is operant at a physiological peak, "at the posterior end of the third ventricle." Which means the gate of the void is annulled, the collective body being thus restored to traverse invisible soils. Perhaps, then, the life span will extend to over 10,000 years, being simultaneous with the plane which is known as the Bramaloka.*

Bellatrix: On Auras, Hydroxyl and Saturn

I want to speak of myself in terms of objective case. Not in terms of seized remainders or proportions, but as an energy writhing on all planes, exponential in extent. In this sense, I am one with Aludra concerning depth of reach, concerning the unlimited origin of cycles. I am concerned with more than the powers of propagation, as something other than nomadic rejoinder. As if I had sired a menacing storm in my own strabismus, knowing myself through waking disorder.

Being of the Southern forms of space I possess what humans would call a briefly contested bravery, as if a skill suddenly ascended from collapsing forms of prayer. This is how my options singe, this is how my power transposes structure. As an atom, I collide and re-release my own atomics as aleatoric ascent. Because we focus on the double globe of the worlds we seek to balance both the individual blood and the contiguous declarations imparted by the grasp of the collective aura. The latter seems to be a blood which now exchanges sickness, which results in the formidable cinders and which occludes the body as immaculate totality so that the human form now leaks with sullen disadvantage. The bones now foster a grammar which signals a general bitterness in the actions. Because we are concerned with this diseased polemic, we know that the fauna wanes, that the sea beds regress.

At one level I read auras, at another, I disintegrate power by understanding its relativity as something other than the plaintive which wanders between phenomena and Ground. Thus, the sky self-implodes through different forms of its own distortion. As if one wandered the range of tragic spiritual geese, of dishonoured quaking grass. This is how energies now distort themselves as forces, as suddenly redacted fumes, working through different forms of surcease. Thus, life becomes coded with invocational debris. All higher modes tend to exhaustion, to cinereous incapacity. Both the general and specific intent of each person is weighed, registered by civilian methodology. Bodies, self-stating themselves as machineries of surcease. And all their structures rally to feed death, to feed a remaindered mucous, in order to create a preterition of things. Now the race loathes a refinement of heaven, so the consequence has been to sully the scrolls of the unseen, to commandeer, to regress intrinsic spirit according to a slate of bones. We understand as suns, that humans now live through clinical deceit, through colluded trans-harmony.

What is the colour of their collective aura?

What is the state of their detonating instants?

Lime?

Javelle water?

Bleach liquor?

I call the above the history of purest nightmare traces.
And what follows are explosive lakes, are in-circulate liminal confusions.

Disharmony compresses. Disharmony becomes key. And so the psyche collects itself with auras of in-seminal nucleation. The nomos then fills with unalterable scarification. With the impermeable, with the viscid, with the nullified. Because the psychic colours clabber, both the specific and general intent of the person is decided by the value according to the international carat. This becomes the standard width of the intellectual persona, with an nth of its flux devalued and made isolate within a milieu of general terminal chromasia. My rays detect the sense of collective glaucescence, fevered, scorched by insomnial lividity. It is like the hatching of sulfuric eggs from a crow. Thus, all the integers are counted in sickened green and stove black. Therefore, the monuments cast no ether, and project no other power than pure physical extrapolation. The mind is thus embrangled in a curious skeptical torrent. The result is that the animating current is rendered by flaws, is enacted by perpetual tumult. These being the laws of damaged cells, inadvertent timing by paralysis. Thereby exposing the crafts to discordance by exterior imposition. A morbid theatrical ironics. A pall which casts its reflection through damage.

I, Bellatrix, as ballistical combinatrics, as copper orange red dust transfusion, as Alice Blue, as Egyptian green, as brilliant milling yellow. Then we come to the Sun as holography as yellow. As bursts which hover, not as replete transmission of ourselves, but as telepathic revivescence, as a calling to the truest levels of the atmosphere. By atmosphere I mean concern with forces which meander by galactic ruin, by intensive Freudian misnomers, the case in point being black fragility as dust. I'm speaking of the plague as rotted symbols, groups of beings being prone to collective zoonosis and not knowing why. And it is known in large measure that the song birds have been wracked by ecological abutment. Because migrations have been distorted, it seems the Sun flies backwards in the genes. The blood flows askew as a technical dissonance, as a bluish enemy within the salt of the collective soma. And because of this dissonance the Sun now subsists as an isolate Dysphasia. Not ceased in itself as regards pure physical emission, but the manner in which its cycles fail, creating in the collective mental colloquia dust of its experiment. Life has become nothing more than basic shadow as quicksand. A loss of depth as contact with expression. There is wavering, the auras de-exist, the subtle takes on a harried assignation.

And here, Mirach, I explore through magnetic duration, through a life of cleansing, living as igniferous crystal. You, Mirach, understand that I know the shifting as transference of auras, of their colours as ripened sand, as flowing instigations. Need I say to you that my aura is blue-white, and tends, when transmixing with hydroxl to take as velocity, an emerald or life-giving arbitrary fuel as connecting spell, as thaumaturgical array, enlivening the field by auricular osmosis. Certainly, not an empirical cross-hatching, but rectilinear disengagement, so the mode of my energies casts itself far beyond the reach of the Earth and its bio-plasmic conditioning. This is not to say that the Sun is constrained, or that the moon does not arc at this level, yet I know in my being that I am casting aura beyond turbulence of the determining or the one condition. It extends light-years across space, and I say this, Mirach, because the Sun loses power 3 million miles beyond Pluto. It is ensnarled, first by its chronic diameter, secondly, by its precise in-locale structured as it is on the nondescript Orion Spur. These are not prejudicial attacks which issue from the unmistakable. I do not seek this or that as heightening, as that which aggrandizes the source which we acknowledge as Bellatrix.

We have all been delivered from a lone imploded star from an unknown aura issued from the multiverse. Our origins are blue, and endless, and strange. Therefore I do not seek to enunciate enigmas, nor do I seek to explode by divisive intent. Riddles are not invoked for the sake of marking implosional calliopes.

In attempting to transmute another spirit to Saturn, I've gathered energies from its namesake in the Saturn Nebula, engaging its inscrutable emerald velocity thereby expanding the salubrious as explorational relation. By giving greenness to Saturn, the core of Enceladus* will spin not unlike the nuclear oceans of the Earth. And by having Enceladus spin in such manner, it will irradiate new auras, allowing species of fish to resurrect, and thrive through inexplicable nucleating. Not only will the grampus and the blackfish ignite again and swelter, but also the pompanos, the thrornback rays, the papagallos, and the perch. Such erupting fecundation will arrive by way of Saturn. The rays from my aura in concert with the penetrant flashes from the Saturn Nebula. Of course my amperage records the green electrics of its body. And at 3000 light-years distant from the Sun my aura sings and leaps, and I, that field of relay which records and erupts as Saturn and New Saturn, and Bellatrix and Earth and again the Sun, and Saturn, and New Saturn.

I am not speaking of a planetoid, or a poisoned band of molecules shifting within the neutral arms of the galaxy, flecked silicates and iron, along with diatomic carbon. Perhaps studded with calcium and graphite. These being the substance of my rotational vacuum, mixed with hydroxyl,* ammonia, and glycine, risen in my instance to an enigmatic ambrosial art. And Saturn as such ambrosial art, reflecting a plaintive solar world, with hydrogen in the depth of its interior, then helium dialectically hovering at the upper range of its regions, combined with ethane and phosphine, and water vapour, with its yellowish clouds, with its light and dark bands, with its atmosphere alit by white and ruddied colour. Its photochemical actions tending to behave as "Jovian white ovals." It is full of regions, and in its metallic hydrogen region the magnetic field is created by the dynamic activity of a rapidly rotating planet. It is "the tilted field in the solar system." Then the particles which consist of "Saturnian aurorae" evoke in my field the poles of Saturnian lightning. As attendant properties of Saturn there exist the retrograde motions of Iapetus and Phoebe, as well as Calypso, and Rhea, and Mimas, and the before described Enceladus. On Earth, Saturn is seen as time through Earthly damage. Let me renounce this glare so that it burns with new beauty. So that it mirrors a thrice infinity, which includes the suns in the Saturn Nebula, and the Sun itself as the Saturn Nebula, and the Earth aligning with these suns, and being included as one of the suns of the Sun.

But we are not absolutes, nor do we play with error in order to provoke mystery. It is that we are looking for greater power than simple ferment. Not strife. Not pleading for inscrutables. Therefore, utopian askewment, plotted impurity, coruscating parallels, imperious para-physical council, all missing. Therefore I do not speak as a single solar flash, or as a signal spawned by corruptive isolation, but as a spirit, as a majestic guardian curiously enkindling eternity within eternity, spinning through my rays intangible proto-eternities. I come to bring ignited spiritus to billions, to transmute through my weavings an inner Microsplanchnics, so unprecedented liberty abounds.

As suns we protest the twin dishonours of arrogance and waste. And we are not didactic as we explore this. As if I were human and weighed a double headed vulture on a transparent scale, as if I could settle its migrant weight around the standards of coalescent claustrophobia, as if its flight ignited mazes and took on the symbol of common instruction. Because we are so removed from common instruction, the flow of each of our qualities as stars burns as gas in an open field like a series of auric flasks creating the unforeseen as symbol. So Iapetus will convey relief for certain forms of human consciousness which wavers. Which means consciousness always fatigued by constricting mental frontality, always sculpting its signals according to meaning or hazard, never quite freed by latent inventiveness to let the lizards roam, to let oneiric exhilaration affect spontaneous interregnums. These being the interregnums where say, Mimas exerts specific example, where say, Enceladus affects the mind with pure medicinal transparence. They will convey to the species certain tenets of the Bramaloka which Aludra has referred to. That sentenant depth which sustains for over 10,000 years, that torrent of symbols which creates triangular doves in the heart. Which creates a certain turbulence as peace, thereby transmuting the very cognizance of neurology, the very Ground which ordinal beings have sometimes listlessly deigned as Theos, Adonai, the Great Spirit. The latter, always portrayed as objectless matter, as some symbol of fish or bread, or official personification of will.

Through astral conveyance Mimas will sweep aside these leanings, these structural myths causing confusion and illness. The haunted rotatoria with energies diverse as Tamarlane and Christ, will become as vanishment, as dazed replicas in-replete with the no-ozone. Marks, dialysis cinders, all vanished.

Sound will be green, bodies will be green, lepers will never again re-occur as symbol of an ailing firmament which befalls us. Again, never comatose resurrection, or electrical populations stumbling as basic drafts through emotion. But energy will re-arise, and take on a fabulous deathlessness as its bearing.

Altair: On Sculpting Hydroxyl

A new lens must pontificate. A new acuity must fuse diamonds in its pointing. The interstellar must be listened to, and then absorbed in the human system as an arcane electrics. What I'm not projecting is the seeming stasis of Mimas with the algid floors of its devastating plains. Like Saturn, it will conduct from the depths of Bellatrix the transformational greenness alchemically spawned in the Saturn Nebula. I call this spiritual hydrology which ignites the empyrean. Not in the form of calloused droppings, but as strange electrical gifts igniting a bluish scent in the system. Which triggers the life force in collecting audacious fuels from the sea.

I focus as panoptical optic, a glass tree staring at the horizon. My focus bearing on an equatorial species whose engrained form of lacking has vanished, and all the starvational cares and ruin subsided. We bring again to the Sun the old Kemetic approach where superstition yields to the health of the forest. The Northern scope, with is clouded mental warrens intuitively cast asunder, masquerading as salt and techne. There are not morals which we seek to adjust to give advantage to inverted neurology as a skill. Because as waves from Bellatrix are ensourced by the Saturn Nebula, they will fuel the inscrutables of Saturn, not through time as affliction, but through complex germinations rising from the genes. As Altair, I shape and focus these genes, these unexplainable levels which approach from Saturn. This being a new biology self-speaking, riotous and in-specific, as the Northern nations waver always seeking in themselves motion triangulate with demise. Because I am conversant with quaking I understand the scent of lawless neutron locales, understanding the violent splendour in certain regions I am not blinded by the spellbound, by the vehement generality which accrues from foreshortened witch hunts. Of course, my essentials speak for erudite arising, as if uranian apotheosis had occurred.

In order for ascensional matters to occur, a greenish hydroxyl will enter from Saturn, and focus its movement in the human pineal system. Then exposure to sleep will provide a new civilian salt. And from this salt will come vapours which will pour from a newly revealed uranian mind not unlike the unsullied energy stored in cellular drafts of plankton. Unlike testing the toxins from cobras a gain will have been made. Not history in the form of abstract biological addenda, but in those levels which hail from the Elysian plane known as the Brahmaloka.*

Alnitak: On Susurrant Conveyance and Yield

We possess original skills. I mean, we as translocated oracles. We mine from our fumes banished in-sonorities, creating from these efforts a series of altered diamonds balanced by a rhythmic aegis.

Within an inner lake on Enceladus there exist groupings of crimson beings absorbing relational oxides from Bellatrix whose skills seem at the surface to work as inoperable ailment. These are not adjusted warrens that they embody. Because they do not speak from radon cinders they can give to human form the power to surrender themselves to the sweeping realias of Aludra, and his rays of anonymous energy. In other words, to become as translatable blindings, working with thought through incendiary patois and crystal. And this crystal, suffused with brief entanglements of oxygen, listens to it-self through the vehicular presence of the aforementioned beings.

Arboreal beacons?

Other modes of extension and gravity?

As they absorb hydroxyl, hydroxyl absorbs itself in the ice. Intangible signals are thus rendered. Then the Sun appears to rise from repressed suggestion. Then we see from our efforts that fauna begins once again to work through cosmic reasoning. Say, as plants, not strictly poised within the conduct of forsythia roots, or as the prone and reactive tremblings of osmunda ferns, but in the manner of transparent ethane models, noiseless, fused with another confluence, fused as auricular waves as inherence.

The Sun

Because I feed on the soul of the being of beings, the Northern regimes have disrupted me, have placed my candle in the form of a wavering flare of disservice. All the species seem ravaged, etherically huddled in a trenchant auricular canyon. The poles now quake, whole continents of beings have dissembled and vanished. Saturn has ensourced me. I've now clarified my depths, knowing my deeper infernos due to anonymity from Aludra. Now, as a force in the midst of healing, I feel surrounded by the glow of Bellatrix.

As the Sun, as RA, I speak as though my aura had re-exploded living in myself as a new heretical subspecies. Knowing that all my auric bodies have allowed me flight, have allowed me arc through the alchemic audition of Mirach. Now I know my name again through a balanced wizardry of forces.

Glossary

Mirach: Girdle/Belt in Andromeda

El Nath: The Butting One

Aludra: The Virgin

Bellatrix: Female Warrior

Altair: "the star"

Alnitak: Belt in Orion

All the above named stars were originally defined by the Moors during the original European Renaissance which lasted in Iberia and Portugal from the 8th to the 15th century. Although the nomen of the above defined stars contains attributions which are female in demeanour in at least three of the cases,but all the lectures were written with a drift towards masculine suasion.

Ernst Mach- One of his best known ideas was Mach's Principle, "concerning the physical origin of inertia." Movement of energy on Earth creates corresponding energy from the stars. The simultaneity of distant action.

Pollux- Yellow giant. 35 light years away. Works "with the intuitive, non-dominant side of the brain." It tunes the mind to thought which has escaped the "three-dimensional processes." It is the closest giant star to Earth.

Deneb- "Blue-white supergiant, 1,600 light years away." Has the "ability to create in people deeper inspired states," allowing an "enhancement of the channeling process to connect to non-physical beings of light."

Beta Centauri- Part of binary system with the star Hadar. It is a "blue-white" sub-giant, 190 light years away. It works with intergalactic elements, and "can significantly increase some people's ability to shift dimensional forms easily."

Aldebaran- Yellow giant, 70 light years away. "The beings associated with

143

this star system have worked with death, loss, and destruction and have come away from it understanding that these are entirely unnecessary."

Antares- "Yellow-orange supergiant, 400 light years away." It enhances the ability "to understand the shadow self, know it, and release certain components of it."

Procyon- A star "which provides a greater acuity of mental functioning that enhances concentration." It can also "enhance the ability to absorb energy directly from plants, the Earth, and the Sun." It "can enhance the direct transference of light into consciousness."

Olympus Mons- The tallest mountain in the solar system. "A volcano two and a half times the height of Everest..."

Kamarupas- In Buddhism; the astral body.

Pantocrater- Christ as the omnipotent "lord of the universe."

3-brained beings- Gurdjieff's term for human beings.

Epimeniades- Cretan poet and philosopher, slept for 57 years in a cave. 7th century B.C.

Pessoa- Great 20th century poet, creator of unparalled heteronyms, who brought the Portuguese language back to prominence after a lapse of over 400 years. Lived 1888-1935.

Alberti- Spanish poet, considered the equal of Lorca, part of the Generation of '27 which also included poets the stature of Salinas and Alexiandre. Also painter. Lived 1902-1999.

Pasqualis Martinez- Spanish alchemist "produced the treatise on the reintegration of beings." It concerns it-self with the "restitution of a lost power and our return to the place from which we were expelled." Lived 1710-1774.

Goa- "Goa's known history stretches back to the third century BCE, when it formed part of the Mauryan Empire, ruled by the Buddhist emperor, Ashoka of Magadha." The original Buddhists were Black and evolved from the Sudra caste in Brahminism. Ashoka was Sudra.

Naim Akbar- Author of *Chains and Images of Psychological Slavery*, and of the essay, "Nile Valley Origins of the Science of the Mind," amongst others. He excoriates with his writings "the limited conception of human potential that one finds in Western science."

d'Avezac- Secretary General of the Geographical Society of Paris, author of *Iles De L'Afrique*. Lived 1800-1875.

Kolarian- Austrics, akin to the Aboriginals. Reached their zenith 15,000 years ago. Known in East/Central India as "Munda and Kolarians. They are smaller Black people not unrelated to the Veddas of Sri Lanka, and the Ainu of Japan."

Indus Valley- Modern day Pakistan was site of "The Indus Valley" civilization which flourished around 2400 B.C. It is the result of the eastward movement of Dravidian peoples who had earlier settled in Arabia. "Indus cities were constructed with a remarkable uniformity, characterized by consistent grid plans of straight streets..." Its port city Lothal was the site of the "oldest artificial dock in the world."

Mohenjo-daro- City in Indus valley civilization located in Sind which is now a province of Pakistan.

Harappa- City in Indus Valley civilization located in "western Punjab," which, along with, the above mentioned Mohenjo-daro, possessed "multiple level houses enhanced by sophisticated wells, drains, and bathrooms complete with toilets."

Indus script- "In spite of extensive research by countless scholars the language remains a mystery."

Costa Rican Puma/ Key Largo Wood Rat- Both members of extinction.

Byblos- Major Phoenician city. Provides "the name for the Christian Bible."

Khaba- Egyptian. Astral or etheric body.

Akhu- Egyptian. Seat of intelligence and "mental perception."

Piankhy- Extricated foreign rulership from Egypt between 720-706 B.C.

Necho- Pharaoh who betrayed Egyptian sovereignty to the Egyptians.

Great Year- the "axis of the earth is tilted about 23 degrees form vertical or true north. The "earth's north axis slowly revolved around true north taking 26,000 years to complete revolution."

BA- "...invisible energy that runs through all visible functions. Essence of all things."

Akashic- Compendium of mystical knowledge compiled on the mystical plane.

Huertas- Fertile land in south-east Spain; produces oranges, pomegranates, figs, almonds, and sugar cane.

Alhambra- Moorish palace in Granada, called the "red house." Constructed between 1248-1354. Houses "the Court of lions," and is considered "one of the most elaborate and important examples of Islamic architecture in the Western World."

Pyramid of Cheops- Cheops is Greek name for Khufu who lived 2600 B.C. Son of King Snefu, he built The Great Pyramid at Giza, it is one of the Seven Wonders of the World still standing.

Walladah- Poet; 11th century; Andalusia. She opened a literary palace in Cordoba. She gained prominence as a poet in a society of males.

Selba/Elvira/Shulayr/Guadix- Regions in Moorish Spain where medicinal herbs grew in abundance.

Lixus- "Ancient city...settled by the Phoenicians in the 7th century B.C. And was later annexed by Carthage."

Almathea- A moon of Jupiter.

Yggdrasil- in Norse mythology, the world tree, the centre of the universe.

"elaborate and theoretical comprehension"- According to Cheikh Anta Diop, Egyptian mathematics was not only operative on the "empirical" plane as was "Babylonian geometry," but had reached the highest arc, and was responsible for the findings of Archimedes, Pythagoras, and Dinostratus.

"accuracy of Egyptian geometry"- Paraphrasing Struve (editor of the "mathematical papyrus of Moscow") Diop states "that the Greeks explicitly admitted that the Egyptians were their masters in the field of geometry which came to Greece from Egypt and not from Babylonia."

Hersetha- Egyptian faculty or "teachers of mysteries." For instance, "Mystery Teachers of Heaven (astronomy and astrology)," "Mystery Teachers of All Lands (geography)."

Double...House- "The Double-White House was the Pharaoh's capital."
Ibn Khaldun- Islamic polymath, historian, mathematician, astronomer, lawyer, whose Mugaddimah, is a philosophy of history cited by Arnold Toynbee as "the greatest work of its kind that has ever yet been created in any time or place."

sporophytes, monocotyls, plankton- plants

bloodroot- produces single white flower in spring.

zoysia/durra- grasses

Delta Ophiuchi- Yellow-orange giant, 95 light years away. "Meditating upon this star can provide some additional stimulation and deeper awareness of the third eye."

Tarazed- Yellow giant 350 light years away. It allows exploration of the deeper powers of the heart. Telepathic "transparence" can be explored.

Rastaban- White giant. 400 light years away. This star helps with sorting out inner conflict.

Iota Orionis- Triple stars. Blue-white, 1,700 light years away. Like the above mentioned stars it is third magnitude.

Adhara- second magnitude star. 650 light years away. This star enhances absorption of minerals and "food in the physical body."

Shamash- Assyrian God of divination, purification, and light. Sun God. Also patron of the law.

Savitar- East Indian solar diety.

Dorado/Caela/Triangulum- Southern Constellations. The Triangulum stated in this context is Triangulum Australe.

Eridanus- Southern constellation. Named after the River Po.

Perseus- Northern constellation. Named after Perseus, the Rescuer or Champion.

Canis Minor- Northern Constellation. Called the Lesser Dog.

Mirzam- Blue-white giant. 700 light years away. Helps with acceptance of the supra-consciousness. Located in Canis Major.

Wezen- White supergiant 2000 light years away. Located in Canis Major. Enhances the ability to see the truth in others.

Alhena- Blue-white binary, "one of which is a subgiant, 100 light years away." In the Northern Constellation Gemini. This star allows individuals to "change modes" and shift contexts.

Zeta Persei- In the Northern Constellation Perseus. "Blue-white supergiant, 1000 light years away." Helps create relaxation in those surrounded by war, and fear, and violence.

Perseus Arm/Scutum Centaurus- The "two major arms" of "the Milky Way."

Orion Spur- Partial arm of "The Milky Way." This is the arm in which the

Sun and the Earth exist.

Heavenly Door- Column of smoke which rose from the Neolithic hearth, analogous to the cosmic axis of the universe.

Zanzibar Red Colobus/ Malayan Tapir/ Spanish Eagle- Under threat of extinction.

rakshasa- A demon of Hindu mythology.

100,000,000 planets- The number of habitable planets in the universe.

Ground- "...unmanifested principle of all manifestation."

Aeshma- Zoroastrian. Assistant of Angra Mainyu. Stirs up fury, wrath, lust and outrage.

Shaitan- Islamic evil spirit. One of 5 types of Jin.

Ravan- In Ramayana, principle antagonist of Rama. Demon king of Lanka.

Angra Mainyu- Zoroastrian God of darkness.

Mirmir- Giant. Sometimes called a water demon. Keeper of a well of wisdom which also mirrors the future.

Ascapart- English giant. 30 feet in height. Space between eyes 12 inches apart.

Galapas- Slain Arthurian giant felled by King Arthur.

Firbauti- Norse giant whose son is Loki, whose wife is the giantess Laufey.

Sri Ramanujacharya- Indian sage who spoke of Hinduism as the eternal religion without "beginning" or "end." This was further enlivened by Sri Aurobindo when he spoke of the eternal religion, or Satanan Dharma, embracing "Science and faith, Theism, Christianity, Mahomedanism and Buddhism and yet is none of these."

paurometabolous- the nymph being almost simultaneous to the adult.

"the sound eye"/"the eye of magic"- In "biological psychiatry," the pineal gland, systemically elicited by the Egyptians.

"...the brain's ventricular system"- the location of the soul within the body. First discovered and explored by the Egyptians. Discussed in the present era by Dr. Richard King.

Enceladus- Moon of Saturn.

Hydroxyl, ammonia, glycine- Interstellar elements.

Mimas- Moon of Saturn. 247 miles wide.

Brahmaloka- The topmost planet of the Universe. In the Bhagavad Gita "we get the information that the number of material planets are only one fourth of that of the spiritual planets."

www.ingramcontent.com/pod-product-compliance
Lightning Source LLC
Chambersburg PA
CBHW051838170626
46807CB00003B/1244